Wanted: McBain

Sheriff Cassidy Yates couldn't believe his eyes when he read the Wanted poster. His ex-deputy, and friend, Nathaniel McBain was both a wanted man and a member of Rodrigo Fernandez's ruthless outlaw gang.

There's nothing worse than a lawman gone bad, and Cassidy knows it's his duty to arrest McBain. But when he finds him, McBain claims the Wanted poster is wrong and his true intention is to infiltrate Fernandez's gang and bring the outlaw to justice.

Is McBain really working undercover? Only one thing is certain: when Cassidy learns the full truth about McBain's plan, it will test to the very limit the strength of his friendship and his duty as a lawman.

Wanted: McBain

I. J. PARNHAM

A Black Horse Western

ROBERT HALE · LONDON

© I. J. Parnham 2005
First published in Great Britain 2005

ISBN 0 7090 7742 4

Robert Hale Limited
Clerkenwell House
Clerkenwell Green
London EC1R 0HT

Typeset by
Derek Doyle & Associates, Shaw Heath.
Printed and bound in Great Britain by
Antony Rowe Limited, Wiltshire

CHAPTER 1

'This ain't the time for heroes,' Nat McBain muttered. 'Just keep those hands above the counter and we'll leave town real peaceful like.'

The bank teller glanced at Nat, then at Spenser O'Connor. He gulped and returned a frantic nod as he shoved the bulging bag across the counter.

'Take it and go,' he whined, his voice shaking as he thrust his hands high.

While keeping his Peacemaker aimed at the teller's chest, Nat hefted the bag in his left hand, then slipped it into the saddle-bag at his feet.

'I'll trust that you ain't holding out on us,' he said.

'And if you are,' Spenser said, his voice gruff behind the kerchief that hid his lower features, 'we'll return for the rest later. And you don't want the Fernandez gang back in town, believe me.'

As the teller closed his eyes and murmured a silent prayer, Nat swung the saddle-bag over his left shoulder and, with Spenser at his side, backed away from the counter, one steady pace at a time.

Nat glared left and right at the customers, who

had been unfortunate enough to be in the bank when they'd raided it. Luckily, most weren't packing guns, and the ones who were didn't meet Nat's gaze as they stared aloft, waiting for this raid to end.

Even so, Spenser edged through the door first, leaving Nat to stand in the doorway and deliver a last glare at the teller, then everyone else.

Outside, Spenser whistled, signifying that nothing was amiss. So, with a last tip of his hat, Nat danced back through the door and slammed it shut behind him.

Despite Nat's warning to the teller, Nat was sure that within a minute he'd raise an alarm. But Nat and Spenser still sauntered to their horses outside the bank, avoiding suggesting to the few people on Bear Creek's main road that they'd raided the bank. Even so, both men kept their kerchiefs over their lower features.

Together, they mounted their horses but, as Nat swung the reins to the side, a warning cry erupted from inside the bank.

'Raid!' the teller shouted, other voices echoing the cry.

Nat and Spenser glanced at each other, both men wincing. Then Nat shook his reins and urged his horse to gallop down the road.

Spenser swung to the side and thrust his gun hand beneath his arm to blast a slug through the bank window, cascading shards of glass into the bank and forcing the customers inside to dive to the floor.

Fifty yards on, Nat kept his gaze set forward. He spurred his horse for more speed, then glanced to his side to ensure that Spenser was beside him, but on failing to see him, he looked over his shoulder.

Outside the bank, Spenser was struggling.

A portly man with more courage than sense had dashed from the bank and had grabbed Spenser's trailing leg. Spenser's horse was prancing round in a circle as Spenser tried to drag his leg away while also regaining control of his mount. But the man had grabbed Spenser's leg in a grip that was so tight it would either drag Spenser from his horse, or drag himself beneath the horse's hoofs. Either way, the delay meant that someone would capture Spenser. So, Nat swung round and hurtled back down the road. He bore down on the man, his gun raised but aimed over the man's head.

Thirty yards away, the man looked up and, in a momentary burst of panic, released his grip of Spenser's leg and staggered back from Nat, falling to his knees in his haste to escape. He glanced up at Spenser, who was prancing his horse from him, then stumbled to his feet and hurtled into the alley beside the bank, his arms wheeling as he fought for more speed.

As the man disappeared from view, Nat pulled his horse to a halt. Then, with Spenser at his side, he glanced in all directions to check that nobody else would act foolishly. But now, everyone who had been on the road had deserted it, leaving doors open and swinging in their haste to hide.

Spenser and Nat exchanged a nod then, side by side, hurtled down the road towards the plains that lay beyond the edge of town. Both men held their guns high and blasted off a volley of high shots, aiming over the roofs of the buildings on either side of the road. Each blast echoed down the road and caused open doors to slam shut and window blinds to hurtle down.

On the edge of town, Nat glanced over his shoulder, then grinned behind his kerchief as their warning shots had the effect they wanted and stopped anybody from emerging out on to the road.

'I thought I'd have to shoot that damn idiot,' Spenser shouted. 'He wouldn't let go.'

'We don't do that.'

'Yeah, but Fernandez's gang sure don't worry about that.'

'I know *they* don't.'

They maintained a furious gallop, not wasting time in looking back and seeing if a pursuit had started.

A mile out of town, at the first incline, they stopped to glance back at Bear Creek and, from this distance, the town was serene. Rooftops captured the glint of sunshine through the afternoon heat-haze. A lazy dust cloud hung over the town.

Spenser grinned and shrugged out from the kerchief that had been over his mouth. He raised his hat, then slapped it against his thigh and let rip with a joyous whoop.

'We did it,' he hollered. 'We sure did. There ain't no pursuit.'

Nat let a smile emerge, but then turned his horse and hurried on down the trail.

'That's what happens,' he shouted over his shoulder, 'when you know Sheriff Ballard ain't around.'

'Yeah,' Spenser said, hurrying to draw his horse alongside Nat's. 'Waiting for him to leave town sure did make a difference.'

'But that was still the easy part.' Nat ripped his kerchief from his face and thrust it in his pocket. 'The dangerous part comes *after* we've escaped.'

At the back of the sheriff's office in Monotony, Sheriff Cassidy Yates stretched even further back in his chair and rocked his legs on to his desk.

'I sure do like this kind of afternoon,' he drawled, suppressing a yawn. 'Nothing happening and no sign of that ever changing.'

Behind the desk to Cassidy's side, Deputy Hearst slipped his hands behind his head and matched Cassidy's posture.

'Well,' he said, 'they don't call this town Monotony for nothing.'

Cassidy chuckled his agreement, then pulled his hat over his eyes, anticipating his siesta.

Within a minute, the first heavy hints of sleep dragged at his eyelids and Cassidy shuffled down into his chair, raising no fight against the pleasant lethargy consuming his body.

But then the door slammed open and crashed back against the wall.

Cassidy winced, but he kept his hat over his face, enjoying the last moments of rest, but the stale odour of sweat and filth invaded Cassidy's nostrils and, with a sigh, he pulled his hat up to peer at the newcomer.

A huge man filled the doorway. The afternoon sun

silhouetted his form and illuminated the surrounding motes of trail dust cascading from his bushy beard. His eyes narrowed, ridging his grime-filled wrinkles.

'Cassidy,' he grunted.

'Marshal Devine,' Cassidy murmured, clattering his feet down to the floor.

Devine grunted and swaggered into the office to stand before his desk.

'So, you still remember me.'

'Ain't seen you in awhile. But you don't forget the man who first hired you.'

Devine glanced at Hearst, who still had his feet resting on his desk, and snorted. 'Hope you ain't gone soft in a quiet town like Monotony.'

'I ain't. But that don't stop us enjoying the quiet.' Cassidy smiled. 'What do you want?'

Devine ripped a roll of paper from his pocket and threw it on Cassidy's desk.

With a questing finger, Cassidy poked the paper open to see that it was a Wanted poster outlining an outlaw's increasingly daring raids.

Then he read the name on the top of the poster and his guts turned to ice.

'Nathaniel McBain,' he murmured, looking up at Devine. 'This has to be wrong.'

'Nope.' Devine spat on the floor. 'Your former deputy's gone bad.'

Cassidy tipped back his hat and rolled to his feet.

'I don't believe he'd . . .' Cassidy paced back and forth behind his desk, staring at the poster. But even when he re-read those terse words, it didn't change the fact that his former deputy, a man he still considered a friend, was an outlaw. He fingered his collar, but it didn't lessen the tightness in his throat. 'And you're bringing him in?'

'Yep.'

Cassidy strode out from his desk and stood before Devine.

'I'll do it.'

'It ain't your duty. He's way out of your jurisdiction.'

Cassidy snorted. 'Since when did you worry about things like that?'

A flashed smile broke Devine's stern features.

'You got yourself a point. But I'm to bring him in. And I will.'

'Strung over the back of your horse, I assume, with a bullet between the eyes?'

Devine licked his lips. 'Most likely. But I ain't here to recruit you. I want more details about Nathaniel. Anything you'd like to tell me before I get him?'

'I could, but listen to me, Devine. Let me do it. He was my deputy. I have to be the one who arrests him.'

Devine looked Cassidy up and down, fingering his beard, a hint of a harsh smile twitching his mouth.

'Because you failed?'

Cassidy glanced away, biting his bottom lip.

'Perhaps.'

Devine nodded. 'There's nothing worse than a lawman who goes bad. But if you ain't telling me anything, I'll pass the word on when I have him.'

'Devine,' Cassidy snapped, then hung his head a moment and softened his voice, 'I have to bring him in – whatever the reason. You can understand that, can't you?'

Devine sneered, then turned on his heel. With slow paces, he headed for the door, but then stopped in the doorway.

'All right,' he said, looking into the road. 'You got one week. Then I'll bring him in.'

'I need more than a week.'

Devine pulled his hat low and paced on to the boardwalk.

'Take it or leave me to it.'

'Then I'll take it,' Cassidy shouted after him.

On the edge of the boardwalk, Devine paused, then headed to his horse, leaving Cassidy to glance at Hearst.

Hearst blew out his cheeks.

'Seems that siesta will have to wait,' he said.

CHAPTER 2

With a bulging saddle-bag resting on his shoulder, Nat McBain headed into the trading post two paces behind Spenser O'Connor.

The rundown building was thirty miles out of Bear Creek, but even without their other reasons for being here, the two days since the raid on the bank had exhausted their supplies.

Spenser stood at the counter and listed their requirements to the post owner while Nat leaned on the counter and peered around.

At the end of the counter, a shifty-eyed man was demolishing the contents of a whiskey bottle with steady determination, but when Nat looked at him, he grabbed the bottle and slouched to a bench. And when he sat, he looked away from Nat.

Surrounded by a protecting wall of dangling harnesses and stacked provisions, a group of men sat on crates in the corner of the post, engaged in earnest conversation. And, from the way they shuffled round to place themselves between Nat and a taller man, Nat reckoned they were guarding him.

From the group, a thick-set man with a wispy red

beard stood and paced to the counter. He shared names with them, Nat learning he was Luther, then peered at the list of provisions Spenser was requesting.

'You want an awful lot of provisions,' Luther said. 'What you want that much stuff for?'

Spenser smiled. 'And what's it to you?'

Luther shrugged. 'Just being right friendly.'

'And so are we. We're just picking up our provisions and then . . .' Spenser glanced at Nat.

'And then,' Nat said, 'we'd like to see someone. Perhaps you might be minded to help us.'

Luther licked his lips and set his feet in a wide stance.

'Ain't interested.'

'You are.' Nat stared at Luther, content to let his silence drag an answer from him.

Luther shuffled from foot to foot, then shrugged. 'Who you talking about?'

'It ain't wise to speak this man's name.'

'I got no idea what you mean.' Luther glanced at the door with a pronounced swing of his head. 'And I ain't interested.'

'We ain't interested in what *you* want. We just want to see what . . .' – Nat glanced around but even though the post owner was still in his back store and the men in the corner weren't close enough to hear him, he edged a pace closer to Luther – 'to see what Rodrigo Fernandez wants.'

Luther winced. 'You got yourself a death wish if you want to see him.'

'But I can see him from here.' Nat glanced over Luther's shoulder at the huddle of men sitting in the corner. 'And now, I'd like to talk to him.'

'You got no—'

'You got trouble, Luther?' a man shouted from the corner of the post.

'Nope,' Luther said. 'Just some idiots searching for . . . for Rodrigo Fernandez.'

As one, the men rose and paced round to face Nat and Spenser, leaving the tallest of them sitting.

Spenser dropped the provisions list on the counter and turned, but Nat just shuffled the saddle-bag to the end of his shoulder.

'We ain't trouble,' Nat said, smiling. 'We just want to talk to Fernandez.'

As the men paced forward to stand five feet before Nat, blocking his route to the door, Luther sauntered to Nat's side and leaned forward, thrusting his face so close to Nat's that his bad breath watered Nat's eyes.

'And why do you reckon I know where he is?'

'Because he headed to Bear Creek yesterday, but then turned away when he discovered the town was bristling with guards. Apparently, someone raided Bear Creek's bank and that spooked the townsfolk.' Nat swung round to stand before Luther. 'We picked up his trail and followed him here.'

Luther stood tall and edged his hand down to his gunbelt.

'And why did you go and do a thing like that?'

Nat patted the bag on his shoulder. 'To give him this saddle-bag.'

'I ain't no messenger. And *you* are leaving.' Luther grinned, as the other men strode a firm pace forward to flank him. 'Either one way, or another.'

15

Nat shrugged. He glanced over his shoulder at Spenser, then dropped the bag at his feet and swung back to slap both hands into Luther's guts. As Luther folded over the blow, he crashed both hands on his back, knocking him to his knees.

Three of the seven standing men charged them, fists raised and held wide. But Spenser slugged the first man to the jaw, knocking him a pace towards Nat, who danced to the side and helped the man on his way with a kick to the rump that slammed him into the counter.

As Spenser squared off to his next opponent, Nat swirled round and threw a punch at the next man to confront him, but the man ducked the blow and leapt at Nat, bundling him back a pace.

Nat pushed a leg wide. He avoided falling and used the leg to pivot and hurl his opponent over his shoulder, using his momentum to crash him into a heap of provisions bags.

Nat heard footsteps pounding behind him and turned to see that Luther had leapt to his feet and was hurling a blow at his face. He swayed back, the blow whistling by his nose, then thundered a short stab to Luther's chin that cracked his head back.

Luther teetered, then fell, collapsing over Spenser's vanquished opponent.

Nat and Spenser glanced at each other, smiling, then swirled round to face the remainder of the men with their fists raised, but it was only to face a line of drawn guns.

'Ain't no need for that,' Spenser said, backing away a pace. 'We just want to see Fernandez.'

'Just go,' Luther muttered from the floor, fingering his jaw, 'while you still can.'

Nat kicked the bag at his feet. 'We're staying until we've given Fernandez this bag.'

'And you ain't—'

'Just take the bag and end this,' a cultured, authoritative voice intoned from behind the row of men.

Although Nat had never heard Rodrigo Fernandez speak, he was sure that the man who had spoken *was* him.

Luther staggered to his feet and moved to grab the bag, but Nat picked it up and threw it to Luther, who caught the bag one-handed then, with a deft swirl of his arm, ripped it open.

Luther's eyes widened and his mouth dropped open, but he covered his surprise with a grunt.

'Anything wrong?' Nat said, raising his eyebrows.

'What you want to give Fernandez this for?'

'That information is for Fernandez's ears only.'

Luther scratched his head, then edged across the post to show the contents of the bag to the nearest man, who tipped back his hat and whistled through his teeth.

This ripple of bemusement encouraged the man at the back to push through the line of men and face Nat.

This man was rangy with piercing blue eyes, a cleft chin and a trim moustache – from the descriptions Nat had obtained, Rodrigo Fernandez.

With his gaze set on Nat, Luther held out the bag. Fernandez glared at the bag a moment then, with it still in Luther's grip, peered inside. He firmed his jaw

17

as he looked at Nat.

'What's this?' he asked.

'Our welcome,' Nat said.

'And what do you want to buy?'

Nat held his hands wide and delivered a short bow. 'Your gratitude.'

Fernandez glanced around the arc of men flanking him, all of whom lined up to peer into the bag. One by one, each man showed his amazement with a variety of whistles and raised eyebrows.

'Then you're mighty odd people.' Fernandez ordered the men to holster their guns, then wandered back to his crate and sat. He pulled a handful of bills from the bag and glanced at them, then dropped them on the nearest crate. 'Where did you get it?'

'Bear Creek's bank.'

'So, it was you.' Fernandez riffled through the bills, then nodded and looked up, a smile that Nat took to be ironic emerging. 'I heard that I had raided the bank.'

'Perhaps the bank reckoned we were so efficient it had to be you.'

'Perhaps. But I heard the raiders claimed to be part of my gang.' Fernandez pushed the bills to one side, then extracted a second handful and frowned. 'And the bank said the raiders stole one thousand dollars. There ain't that much here.'

'Yeah, it's just under five hundred. But you can't trust banks.'

'You can't.' Fernandez shuffled the bills into a pile, then sat back and gestured at the money with an open palm. 'And what do you expect *me* to do with this?'

'I understand you distribute any money that comes to you around your men fairly.'

'I do.'

'Then distribute it.'

Fernandez narrowed his eyes. 'And do you two get a share?'

Nat and Spenser edged a pace closer to each other and, in unison, smiled.

'I guess that's the question we're here to ask.'

'You did well to raid Bear Creek's bank. And you've intrigued me with your method of getting my attention.' Fernandez favoured Nat with a huge smile, then let it disappear in a moment. 'But I ain't looking for more help. Leave.'

Fernandez gestured for Luther and the other men to join him and, with studied finality, they sat and turned their backs on Nat and Spenser.

'We'll go,' Nat said. 'But that money is just the start.'

With a hand cupping his mouth, Fernandez whispered to Luther, who swirled round on his crate to face Nat.

'You heard Fernandez,' he grunted. 'You got his gratitude, but that'll die if you don't leave – as will you.'

'But I reckon you're planning to raid the gold shipment that's heading to Bear Creek next week. I've heard that it'll be worth around ten thousand dollars, and we want in on it.'

'Talk like that is dangerous.' Luther narrowed his eyes. 'Go!'

'Even though we have inside information that'll

make that raid flow as smoothly as our raid on Bear Creek's bank did?'

'And we ain't—'

'Luther,' Fernandez said, laying a hand on Luther's arm, 'get crates for these men. I'd like to hear more about this *inside* information.'

'So,' Deputy Hearst said, 'who is Nathaniel Mc-Bain?'

Sheriff Cassidy Yates sensed that Hearst was looking at him, but he stared straight ahead with his jaw set firm.

'He's just an outlaw we'll bring to justice.'

'I know you got plenty of problems, but you have to tell me what I'm facing sometime.'

Cassidy sighed. For three hours, they'd ridden west from Monotony. And he'd never gone that long without explaining the details of his mission to his deputy.

But in this case, he hadn't trusted himself to speak.

'I'm sorry,' he said, then coughed to clear the gruffness from his voice. 'Nathaniel McBain was my deputy for a few months before I came to Monotony.'

'You're mighty unhappy because of someone who worked for you for just a few months?'

Cassidy rode on for another fifty yards then snorted.

'Nathaniel was my first deputy. So, I guess he was also my first attempt to judge character as a lawman.'

'That don't make it your fault that he went bad.'

'Perhaps.' Cassidy turned in the saddle to face Hearst. 'But he came from an outlaw family and I reckoned I'd persuaded him to make the right choices in life.'

'But then he left?'

'He did. At the time, I wasn't concerned. He became a bounty hunter, and I reckoned he'd be successful. But I never expected him to become a wanted man. And now, nobody can tell me that his failure ain't my failure.'

'I can understand why you want to bring him in, but Devine could do it. Nobody escapes that lawman.'

'You're right. But despite Nathaniel's mistakes, he must have a reason why he's doing what he's doing. And I want to hear him explain himself.'

'I can see that. But the last sighting of Nathaniel was in Lincoln and then he went even further west. That's way out of our territory. And we got no arrest warrant and we got no right to head into another lawman's territory and—'

'And I know that,' Cassidy snapped, then lowered his voice. 'I know that, but if Devine gets him, he'll end up dead. I can't let that happen.'

Hearst coughed and shuffled in the saddle, then turned to Cassidy.

'Got to ask you – how far will you go to protect Nathaniel in the name of an old friendship?'

Cassidy smiled. 'Relax, Hearst. I won't forget my duty. I just want to know why he went bad.'

'And when you find that out?'

Cassidy firmed his jaw. 'I'll arrest him.'

CHAPTER 3

'I am right,' Spenser said, glancing at a huddle of men standing outside the stable. 'Everyone *is* looking at us.'

Nat glanced at the men, but they were all either looking into the stable, or chatting amongst themselves.

'Quit worrying,' he said, with a short laugh. 'Ballard left town an hour ago and we've changed our horses and our clothes. So, unless you wrap a kerchief over your mouth and start firing in all directions, nobody will recognize us.'

Spenser provided a reluctant nod. 'Yeah, but that don't stop me looking for people who might recognize us.'

Nat chuckled, but as they rode into Bear Creek at a walking pace, Spenser still peered at every building and at every person they passed.

At the bank, they dismounted. Nat looked at the boarded window, cocking his head from side to side as he feigned being surprised at seeing the broken window for the first time. Then he shuffled the saddle-bag on to his shoulder and, with Spenser at his side, headed to the door.

But two bulky guards in red coats paced from the doorway to stand before them. One guard glared at him and held out an imperious hand.

Nat furrowed his brow, but then saw the direction of the guard's gaze and unwound his gunbelt. Along with Spenser, he handed the belt to the guard and moved to enter the bank, but the second guard stood before him.

'The bag,' he grunted, 'open it.'

'Glad to see this bank is secure,' Nat said, opening the bag.

'Yeah, well there was a ... some trouble here earlier.' The guard gulped on seeing the bag's contents. He beckoned the other guard to join him and, together, they peered into the bag then, as one, blinked hard.

They backed away two paces from Nat and murmured to each other. Then the first guard held a hand to the side, encouraging him to enter.

'This way, sir,' he said, his voice light and a smile appearing. 'I'll take you straight to Mr Gillespie.'

Nat and Spenser exchanged a smile, then followed the guard inside. Nat strode across the bank with his back straight and his chin aloft, but even so, he avoided looking at the teller, the most likely person in the bank to recognize them. But if the teller even noticed them enter the side room, Nat wasn't aware of it.

Isaac Gillespie, the senior clerk, was sitting behind a desk. He grunted his displeasure in letting anyone disturb him, but the guard dashed to his side and whispered in his ear.

In a moment, a huge smile appeared and Isaac strode out from his desk, his hand outstretched. He clasped Nat's hand in a clammy grip then moved on to Spenser, almost shaking both men's arms out of their sockets.

'I'm Isaac Gillespie, but you can call me Isaac,' he said, eyeing the saddle-bag. 'Now, what can I do for you two gentleman?'

'We're here to do something for you, Isaac,' Nat said.

'Excellent. Would you like a drink, gentleman? Or perhaps you'd prefer a cigar, or maybe I could have—'

'We have everything we need.' Nat held out the bag to Isaac. 'But you might want this.'

Isaac gleamed and opened the bag. 'I'll get Jim to count this out, but I reckon there's around . . .' – Isaac appraised the wads of bills in the bag, mouthing to himself – 'five hundred dollars here. A deposit for two new customers, I presume?'

'You're good at your job. That *is* around five hundred, but the exact amount ain't important to us.'

'Five hundred dollars and you're not concerned about . . .' Isaac dropped the bag on his desk and clasped his hands before him, his eyes wide and shining. 'You must be wealthy men, indeed. And I must say, you've come to the right place. We specialize in providing a service for men of substance.' Isaac lowered his voice. 'It isn't important, but what do you do?'

'We're bounty hunters.' Nat watched a momentary frown invade Isaac's features before the smile returned. 'And we're after Rodrigo Fernandez.'

Isaac tipped back his hat. 'Bring him in and everyone within a thousand miles will be delighted.'

'We intend to. And we want your help with some information on cash shipment dates and details of the gold—'

Isaac raised a hand. 'I don't want to offend my new customers, but nobody will learn that information.'

'Even when they're as good as we are?'

'Clearly, you are good.' Isaac patted the bag, then withdrew a wad of bills. 'But not even then.'

'And even when they return your money to you?' Nat grinned.

'Ours?' Gillespie intoned, staring at the bills in his hand.

'I'm sorry we didn't get it all back. But we tracked Fernandez's gang and ambushed a straggler. He got away, but we reclaimed this.' Nat glanced at Spenser, who paced forward to stand beside him. Both men smiled. 'We specialize in providing a service to banks of substance.'

Isaac patted the wad of bills against an open palm.

'And you've done that already.' Isaac rubbed his chin. 'I'm not sure what reward I can offer. The bounty on Fernandez is for—'

'We ain't interested in a reward for getting a job half done,' Nat said, raising a hand, then sat on the edge of Isaac's desk. 'We're just interested in the ten thousand dollar reward for bringing in Fernandez. And with your help, we can end your problems with him forever. We might even get back the other half of that stolen cash.'

Isaac slapped the wad of bills into the bag and stared at the bag a moment, then nodded.

'Being as you put it that way, I guess we could help each other.'

'Now,' Sheriff Ballard muttered, slamming his hands on his hips, 'why might I be interested in that?'

'Because he's a wanted man,' Cassidy said, waving the Wanted poster at Ballard. 'Nathaniel McBain was last seen in Lincoln and—'

'I didn't mean that,' Ballard shouted, his voice echoing through his office as he slammed a fist on his desk. 'I mean why is a lawman coming into *my* office and telling *me* how I should run *my* investigations in *my* town?'

Cassidy looked to the ceiling a moment, taking calming breaths, then glanced at Hearst, who returned a slow shake of his head and an I-told-you-so frown.

'I'm *not* telling you how to run your town. For the last five days, we've followed Nathaniel's trail, and now that we're in Bear Creek, I'm here to tell you I don't want a confrontation.'

Ballard wandered round his desk.

'You are, are you?' With his face set in a fixed smirk, Ballard leaned back against the desk and folded his arms. 'That is so kind of you. I'm so mighty obliged for your generosity that I'll let you run my office.'

Cassidy gritted his teeth against the heavy sarcasm.

'I have enough trouble running my own office.'

'And you run Lincoln well, do you?'

'I'm from Monotony.'

'You ain't even Lincoln's sheriff!' Ballard shook his head. 'I suppose you went there and ran that sheriff's county for him. Then you got bored and came here.'

'No. I just know Nathaniel McBain, and I can help you capture him.'

'I know how you can be helpful.' Ballard pushed himself from the desk and paced towards Cassidy, stopping two paces before him, then pointed to the door. 'You can turn round, walk out this office, get on your horse, ride out of Bear Creek, and keep on riding until you reach your own town – Morbid, was it?'

Cassidy backed away a pace, his jaw aching from the permanent smile he'd forced himself to adopt while talking to Ballard.

'Monotony. You don't think you need my help, but I'm not leaving town.' Cassidy removed the smile. 'So, when I leave your office, consider putting your concerns aside so that we can slam a wanted man in jail.'

Ballard folded his arms. 'I've done that. And when I catch the rest of the Fernandez gang, I'll bring Nathaniel McBain in as well, but the likes of him are way down my list of wanted men.'

'Nathaniel's with the Fernandez gang?' Hearst said, pacing to Cassidy's side.

For the first time, Ballard turned his sneering gaze on Hearst.

'I've only just learned that. But that proves you're

useless. You claim you have information, yet you don't even know important details like that.' Ballard slapped a hand on Hearst's shoulder, spun him round, and pointed him towards the door. 'Just get out.'

'Yeah, but—'

Cassidy raised a hand, silencing Hearst.

'Come on,' he said. 'We'll leave Sheriff Ballard to consider using us.'

Ballard turned his back on Cassidy first. 'Leave town now and save yourself a long wait.'

Cassidy glared at Ballard's back, then turned on his heel and strode outside. On the boardwalk, he waited for Hearst, but when he emerged, the deputy stared up and down the road, not meeting Cassidy's gaze.

Cassidy smiled. 'Obliged to you for not saying you knew that would happen.'

'Didn't think it would help none.' Hearst shrugged. 'But it don't stop me wondering what we'll do now that Ballard has stopped us going after Nathaniel.'

'That meeting changed nothing. Ballard said exactly what I expected him to say. But I had to see him first; it was the right thing to do.'

'I can see that, but time's running out before Devine comes for Nathaniel, and Ballard won't change his mind any time soon.'

'He won't. But I did learn some valuable information that I didn't know before.'

Hearst nodded. 'That Nathaniel has joined Rodrigo Fernandez. But that'll make it a whole lot harder for anyone to get him.'

'Maybe. But I prefer to think it gives us a start to our investigation.'

'But Ballard said we can't do anything.'

Cassidy rubbed his jaw as he licked his lips, his gaze averted from Hearst.

'Ballard only said we couldn't run his town for him or arrest anyone. He never said we couldn't investigate.'

'I reckon he meant that . . .' Hearst considered Cassidy's smile. 'I suppose asking a few questions won't do no harm.'

Cassidy nodded, then peered along the road until his gaze alighted on the only saloon in town.

'And I know where we'll start.'

'Drinking won't help none.'

'It won't. But Ballard told me two interesting facts about Nathaniel. And I reckon the saloon is where we can use that information.' Cassidy headed off the boardwalk.

Hearst hurried on to join Cassidy. 'Ballard only told us one thing: that he'd just learned that Nathaniel had joined Fernandez.'

'Yeah. And that's two pieces of information.'

'But I don't see . . .' Hearst sighed. 'Cassidy, I just don't understand your hunches these days.'

Cassidy patted Hearst's shoulder as he paced on to the boardwalk outside the saloon.

'Nathaniel would have known what I meant, and he went bad.' Cassidy slapped a hand on the batwings. 'I prefer you just the way you are.'

'Obliged,' Hearst murmured. 'Or at least I reckon I am.'

CHAPTER 4

Deputy Hearst raised his third whiskey to his lips, then lowered it.

'We've been here an hour,' he said, 'and you still ain't told me how drinking whiskey will help us to find Nathaniel.'

Cassidy turned from the bar and cradled his whiskey glass against his chest as he glanced around the saloon.

This early in the afternoon the usual low-life dregs were littering up the room, but Cassidy had already identified the man he wanted to talk to and was waiting for the right moment to approach him.

The dirt-streaked and unkempt man was down to the last dregs in his whiskey bottle and, from his red eyes and shaking hands, Cassidy reckoned he'd consumed the whole bottle this afternoon.

But then the man threw the bottle over his shoulder. As the bottle rattled to a halt in the corner of the saloon, he tipped his hat to a jaunty angle and stood from his table. He stumbled, rocking the table to the side, then, with a shoulder thrust down, wandered round the table.

'You know how I work,' Cassidy said, turning from his studious appraisal of this man. 'I get hunches, and I back them. And that hunch is heading to the bar right now.'

Cassidy leaned on the bar as the man staggered a wending path to the bar and stumbled against it.

'Bartender,' the man said, his voice slurred. He thumped his fist on the bar. 'More whiskey.'

'You're mighty full of good cheer today, Dewey,' the bartender said, smiling. But he replaced the smile with a harsh frown. 'But you don't get credit from me.'

'I can pay.' Dewey waved his arms above his head, stumbling himself back a pace so that he had to grab the bar to stop himself falling over. 'Just set 'em up, and I'll drink 'em.' He dragged a dollar bill from his pocket and slapped it on the bar.

The bartender eyed the bill, then poured a large whiskey from a full bottle and pushed both across the bar to Dewey.

Two yards to Dewey's side, Cassidy raised his glass to his lips, then lowered it and snorted a laugh.

With one bleary eye open and the other eye closed, Dewey paced round on the spot and glared at Cassidy.

'What you findin' funny?' he muttered, wafting a great breeze of stale whiskey-breath into Cassidy's face.

'Just enjoying seeing a man with money,' Cassidy said, blinking to clear his watering eyes. 'You win it in a poker game?'

'And what's it to you where I got me money?'

'I like a game of poker myself and if there's one going, I'd like to know where to go.'

'No poker.' Dewey pushed himself from the bar, then waved his hand in a dismissive gesture. 'And you ask too many questions for my likin'.'

Cassidy watched Dewey stagger across the room, lurch into his table, right it, then finally fall into his chair. Cassidy turned and downed his drink then patted Hearst's chest with the back of his hand. With his back straight and keeping his gaze from Dewey, he wandered outside.

Cassidy headed across the road towards the store, not waiting for Hearst to join him, then turned and leaned on the rail.

At a steady pace, Hearst joined him and matched his posture.

'What do we do now?' he asked.

'We wait for Dewey to drink the last of his money away.'

'And then?'

'And then we start our investigation.'

The sun had set when Dewey left the saloon and stumbled off the boardwalk to land in a sprawled heap. He levered himself to his feet, then pointed down the road and set off on a snaking route.

Outside the store, Cassidy and Hearst straightened and, with a last glance along the road to confirm nobody was looking at them, they wandered across the road and followed him, keeping on the board-walk.

Dewey was whistling tunelessly and raising his hat

to every passing person. None of these people returned as much as a glance, but that didn't dampen Dewey's good spirits as he hailed everyone, whistled, sang, and enjoyed his good fortune.

At the edge of town, he reached his horse, a mangy bay and, on the fifth attempt, rolled into the saddle. He immediately slumped forward and was on the brink of tumbling to the ground, but the horse, with practised skill, set off out of town, rocking Dewey back in his saddle.

Cassidy watched until he was sure of his direction, then turned and headed back to his horse.

At a walking pace, he and Hearst headed out of town, following Dewey, but keeping as far back as they could while still keeping him in sight.

Four miles out of town, Dewey's horse stopped outside the wrecked remnants of a house that consisted of three walls, all crumbling, and cloth dragged over the burnt roof timbers.

For a full minute, Dewey sat in the saddle but then the horse nudged forward, awakening him from his drink-fuelled slumbers.

Dewey started and half-rolled, half-fell from the saddle, then wandered into the shell of the house. As he disappeared from Cassidy's view, Hearst shook his head and glanced at Cassidy.

'I still don't see how that wretch can lead us to Rodrigo Fernandez or Nathaniel McBain, unless you plan to ask his horse. It knows the way around better than he does.'

Cassidy laughed. 'Dewey will lead us to them because he is a wretch.'

Hearst tipped back his hat. 'I'm sorry, Cassidy. I don't see it.'

'Dewey has money, and from his determined effort to drink himself senseless in the saloon, he doesn't have money that often. And he got it recently.' Cassidy turned to Hearst. 'And I ask myself how.'

'Well, he didn't win it in no poker game.' Hearst rubbed his chin. 'So, from the look of him, I reckon he stole it.'

'Perhaps, but Dewey doesn't strike me as resourceful enough to steal, and I have a hunch.' Cassidy tugged on the reins and pulled his horse from the trail. 'And I'll back my hunch that he got that money from a source that'll lead us to Nathaniel.'

Hearst shook his head, but then followed Cassidy.

'Either way, Cassidy, your hunches just get stranger.'

Cassidy paced his horse to the house and dismounted. With Hearst two paces behind him, and still shaking his head, he lifted the cloth wall and peered into the shell of the house.

In the corner of the building, Dewey was sprawled on his back beneath a threadbare blanket and ripping out great rasping snores.

Cassidy gestured for Hearst to guard Dewey's escape route, then paced into the house. He stood over Dewey and tapped his foot against his ribs with an insistent rhythm.

Lost in sleep, Dewey muttered and batted forlornly at Cassidy's foot as if it were an irritating bug, but with each blow, Cassidy swung his foot further and further back until Dewey shrugged away.

'What you want?' he whined, his voice slurred. He peered up at Cassidy with his eyes narrowed.

Cassidy paced round so that the dying remnants of light on the western horizon lit his face.

'To talk to you.'

'I remember you.' Dewey clapped his mouth open and closed, then settled down. 'Don't care where. Go away.'

'We met in the saloon.'

'Did I buy you a drink?' Dewey's voice faded as his eyes closed.

'Nope.'

'Well, it's too late.' Dewey's shuffled on to his side. 'I drank all the money away.'

'And where did you get that money?' Cassidy glared down at Dewey, but snores were already ripping from his throat. Cassidy kicked his leg. 'I said, where did you get that money?'

Dewey gurgled a last snore, then opened an eye and glared at Cassidy's foot until he stopped kicking him.

'Perhaps I do remember you. You wanted a poker game. You find one?'

'Nope.'

'Then what you want with me?' Dewey whined, running fingers through his bedraggled hair. 'I told you I didn't get the money in no poker game.'

'But you didn't tell me where you *did* get the money.'

'And I ain't.' Dewey shook a fist at Cassidy. 'So, go away. You got nothin' on nothin' I done.'

Dewey rolled over on to his other side, turning his

back on Cassidy, and grabbed his blanket, then pulled it up to his chin.

Cassidy gestured to Hearst, who paced to Dewey's other side, but Dewey shuffled round to lie on his front, even drawing his legs up.

Hearst and Cassidy exchanged a smile. Then Hearst grabbed Dewey's blanket and ripped it from him.

'Answer the question,' he said.

Dewey lay a moment, reaching behind his back for the blanket with his eyes clamped tight, but when his questing hand couldn't find it, he crawled to the wall and rolled over. He propped himself against the wall and held out his tattered jacket.

'I got no money. I own nothin' but these clothes and me horse, and you won't get much of anythin' for either.' Dewey glanced at Cassidy and Hearst in turn, receiving only steely glares. 'Ah, come on, people. I wouldn't be livin' here if I had anythin' to steal.'

'But we don't want to steal *anything*,' Hearst said, leaning down to place his face a foot from Dewey's. 'We just want to know where you got that money.'

Dewey narrowed his eyes. 'What have people said?'

Hearst stood tall and glanced at Cassidy, who shrugged.

'Nothing,' Cassidy said, 'but that leaves me to surmise, and I got a theory as to how you got it.'

'How?' Dewey squeaked.

'You sold information. And in return, you got some drinking money.'

Dewey gulped, then rubbed a shaking hand over his mouth.

'Don't know nothin' about that.'

Cassidy nodded and half-turned from Dewey.

'Then I'm sorry. I must have got it wrong. I'll just head back to the saloon and tell everyone my theory that Sheriff Ballard came into some mighty interesting information today about Rodrigo Fernandez.' Cassidy glanced at Hearst, who returned a nod. 'And I'll wonder aloud whether you sold him that information.'

Dewey slammed his eyes shut so tightly that his face almost caved in.

'Talk like that ain't fair on no one.'

'You're right. I reckon Fernandez won't ask too many questions before deciding it's true.' Cassidy glanced at Hearst. 'Come on. We got a saloon to visit.'

Dewey rolled to his feet and stumbled to Cassidy's side. He laid a shaking hand on Cassidy's arm, his eyes watering and beseeching.

'And if I tell you the truth, what will you do?'

Cassidy favoured Dewey with his friendliest smile.

'I'll leave you alone.'

'What assurance I got?'

'None.' Cassidy ripped his arm from Dewey's grip and took a determined pace towards his horse.

'Don't go!'

Cassidy strode four long paces, then turned and raised his eyebrows.

'I'm listening.'

Dewey took a deep breath. 'I *did* sell Sheriff Ballard some information.'

'And what was it?'

Dewey lowered his head, muttering under his breath, then turned his watery gaze back on Cassidy and raised his chin.

'Know this,' he said, his voice stronger than before, 'no matter what you threaten me with, I ain't sayin' nothin' that could make Fernandez think I sold information about him.'

'But I'm not looking for Fernandez; I'm looking for Nathaniel McBain. And apparently, he's just joined Fernandez.'

Dewey nodded. 'I told Ballard everythin' I know about him. And that ain't nothin' more than the news that McBain and another man joined Fernandez last week.'

Cassidy sauntered towards Dewey, who backed away until he stumbled into the wall. Cassidy loomed over him then darted his hand to his jacket pocket, Dewey flinching, but it was only to extract a dollar bill, which he tucked into Dewey's top pocket.

Dewey patted his pocket. 'Obliged for the money, but I'd be more obliged if you didn't tell anyone about this.'

'I won't, but you've told me nothing new. The money is for what you're about to do.' Cassidy grinned. 'You're taking a message to Nathaniel McBain.'

Dewey's mouth fell open. Then he closed it with a shaking hand and rubbed his bristled cheeks.

'I can't do that.'

Cassidy shrugged. 'Then I'll tell everyone what you did.'

'You can, you can,' Dewey babbled. 'But I still can't

take no message. Nobody knows I sell information to Ballard. Fernandez tolerates me bein' around – I guess he reckons I'm just a whiskey bum stinkin' up the bar.'

'He must be a perceptive man.'

'He is, and if I pass on a message to someone near to him, he'll figure out what I've been doin' and I'll be dead by sundown.'

'Quit worrying, Dewey. This message won't get you killed.' Cassidy smiled and laid a friendly hand on Dewey's shoulder. 'Nathaniel won't tell Fernandez about it. And the message is short. In fact, it's just one word.'

CHAPTER 5

'How much longer will he be?' Spenser asked.

Nat leaned back on his crate and glanced around the trading post. For two hours, they had waited. Several of Fernandez's men had already entered, acknowledged them, but not drawn them into their discussions.

'Fernandez's coming,' Nat said. 'Just be patient.'

Spenser tapped his fingers on the top of the barrel before him with an insistent rhythm.

'I am patient. I just don't like waiting.'

Around the trading post, men shuffled as the door opened, but then returned to their drinks, ignoring the portly, downtrodden man who slouched to the counter.

Spenser glanced at Nat and raised his eyebrows.

'Dewey Wade,' Nat whispered, 'I think.'

Nat hunched over his drink, but from the corner of his eye, he saw Dewey glance at him before ordering a whiskey. Nat ran his glass through his fingers waiting, and, sure enough, Dewey shuffled across the room and slumped down on a crate beside him.

With his shoulders hunched, Dewey glanced

40

around the trading post, but nobody was looking at him, so he pulled the crate closer to Nat and cleared his throat.

'I got me a message for a Nathaniel McBain,' he murmured.

'I answer to *Nat* McBain.'

'Message is the same no matter what you answer to.' Dewey gulped back his whiskey and took a deep breath, then wiped his quivering mouth with the back of his shaking hand, stilling it.

'Just give me the message,' Nat snapped. 'I won't tell anyone.'

'Obliged. The message is . . .' Dewey glanced over Nat's shoulder and peered around the post again, then leaned forward and lowered his voice to a whisper. 'The message is a name – Cassidy.'

Nat's guts grumbled, but he bit back his shock and shot out a hand to grab Dewey's collar.

'Who gave you the message?'

'I'm just a messenger,' Dewey whined, struggling, but failing, to free himself from Nat's grip. 'That's all I am. And now, I'm leavin'.'

'You're going nowhere until you tell me who gave you the message.' Nat pulled Dewey's collar tight, but Dewey firmed his jaw and clamped his mouth tight. 'Was it Cassidy Yates?'

Dewey's eyes rocked from side to side. Then he shrugged.

'I don't rightly ask names when they ain't—' Dewey gulped as Nat flared his eyes and pulled him forward, the action drawing the interest of several men by the door.

41

'Talk.'

'I've had enough of this,' Dewey whined. He lowered his voice to a resigned whisper. 'It was him.'

Nat released Dewey's collar and threw him back on his crate.

'You don't sit with us!' he snapped, raising his voice and throwing back his hand, as if to slap Dewey's face. 'We're mighty particular about the company we keep.'

Dewey furrowed his brow, but then his eyes glazed as he realized that Nat was giving him an excuse for their confrontation and jumped to his feet.

'And I'm particular about who I sit with, too. I wouldn't—' Dewey threw his arms before his face as Nat raised a fist, then pointed to the counter. 'I'll stand over there.'

Dewey scurried to the counter, his plight raising a chuckle from several men around the post.

Nat dismissed Dewey from his mind and stared at his glass. Spenser was looking at him, waiting for an explanation, but five minutes passed before Nat had ordered his thoughts sufficiently to turn to him.

'Sorry, Spenser,' he said, 'but we have to abandon our plans. Cassidy Yates is close.'

'Cassidy was your former boss?' Spenser leaned closer to Nat and considered him until he nodded. 'Then I ain't surprised that he's come for you. But that's no reason to be nervous. Once we're in Fernandez's gang, we'll be safe. And besides, the raid is in two days, and if Cassidy is closing on you, he ain't got the time to track you down.'

'But I know how Cassidy works. And he ain't just

close.' Nat glanced over his shoulder at the door, then turned back to Spenser. 'He'll walk in here within the hour, perhaps within the next minute.'

Spenser glanced over his shoulder at Fernandez's men who were sitting around the post.

'Then he's an idiot.' With an outstretched finger, Spenser tipped back his hat and sat back on his crate. 'But if you're that worried, we can leave. We don't need to be here when Fernandez arrives. We have information he needs, and he can find us.'

'You don't understand. Cassidy wants me to run. He's watching the post, waiting for me to leave.'

'You can't know that. It took us months to infiltrate Fernandez's gang. Cassidy can't know you're here that quickly.'

'He can. He found Dewey, just about the only person who could give me a message.'

Spenser shook his head. 'The message was only his name. You're reading too much into it.'

'I'm not. The message wasn't important. Cassidy just wanted to find me. So, he followed Dewey until Dewey led him to us. And that means he's outside, right now.'

Spenser patted Nat's shoulder. 'Quit worrying. We've been through plenty together. We'll see off another lawman.'

'But we won't. Cassidy ain't just another lawman.'

Spenser snorted. 'He can't be that good.'

'He is. But I don't mean that. Cassidy is . . . was my friend. And when he deputized me, I promised to always help him. So, I won't take him on. And you know me, Spenser – I never go back on my word.'

Spenser snorted. 'You did that when you stopped being a lawman and joined me.'

'I rejected the lawman life: I didn't reject Cassidy.'

Spenser rolled forward on his crate to rest his hands on his knees. He considered Nat, shaking his head, but then the door creaked open and he pulled Nat back to lean against the pile of bags behind them.

'Company,' he whispered, then stared over Nat's shoulder, watching, from the steady footfalls, two men pace across the post. 'Suppose they got the look of lawmen. The older man is—'

'I don't need a description,' Nat murmured, looking to the ceiling, his guts clenching from thinking about a confrontation that he hoped he'd never have to face. 'It's Cassidy.'

'What you want?' the post owner asked.

'Provisions.' The authoritative voice wasn't Cassidy's and, with hope fluttering in his chest, Nat edged forward.

From the corner of his eye, he glanced at the counter. He winced. The man who'd spoken was facing him and wasn't Cassidy, but the man with his back to him was.

With a glance at Nat, Dewey pushed himself from the counter and headed outside, his gaze averted from Cassidy.

Cassidy watched Dewey leave, then turned to the post owner. But Luther rolled to his feet and paced across the post to stand beside him.

'You want an awful lot of provisions,' he said.

'Got an awful long journey ahead of us,' Cassidy

said, then smiled. 'Sooner we get them, the sooner we'll be on our way.'

Luther stared at Cassidy a moment, then nodded and turned but, as he left the counter, he glanced at Nat and Spenser, who were both sitting as far back into the mess of bags as they could. He stared at them, a sly smile on his lips as he appraised their attempts to hide from the newcomers.

Then Luther swung back to face Cassidy.

'And you don't want anything else?'

Cassidy glanced at the list in the post-owner's hand.

'Nope. Reckon Hearst's ordered everything we need.'

'And you ain't searching for anyone?'

'Not that I know of.'

'And I reckon you are,' Luther grunted and squared off to Cassidy.

With Luther raising his voice, four men pushed themselves from the wall and paced across the room to surround Cassidy and Hearst.

The man who stood nearest to Hearst strode forward a firm pace, slammed his hands on his hips, and leaned forward to glare deep into Hearst's eyes.

Hearst glanced at Cassidy, who shook his head, and Hearst backed away a pace. But Luther edged his hand towards his holster, forcing Cassidy to swing round and knock his hand away.

Within seconds, all five men had leapt on Cassidy and Hearst, pushing them back against the counter.

Four more men peeled from their crates and spread out to stand on the edge of the fight, searching for an opening, but so many men surrounded Cassidy and Hearst that they couldn't deliver a single blow.

Nat jumped to his feet and took a pace towards the fight, but Spenser grabbed his arm and pulled him back.

'This is where we leave,' he said.

Nat shrugged Spenser's hand away. 'I got to stop this.'

Spenser slammed a firmer hand on Nat's shoulder. 'Leave. Now.'

Nat opened his mouth to shout his refusal, but by the counter, the tangle of fighting men parted as Cassidy fought his way out.

For just a moment Nat and Cassidy's gazes locked. Then Luther shoved Cassidy to the floor and two more men dived on his back, knocking him flat.

With his guts rumbling at his actions, Nat lowered his head and let Spenser lead him to the back exit.

Outside, Nat heard the shouting and the crashing from inside the post as the fight gathered momentum, but he gritted his teeth against the noise and shuffled away. With a last look at the post, he mounted his horse.

Spenser mounted his own steed and, without a backward glance, they rode to the trail, then veered off to the hills, heading for their encampment.

Even over the clop of his horse's hoofs and with the distance growing, Nat reckoned he could hear the thud of fist on flesh, and when he closed his eyes, he reckoned he could see Cassidy's gaze piercing into him.

'Faster,' Spenser shouted.

'I'm not,' Nat murmured. 'I ain't proud of running.'

'You ain't a lawman now.' Spenser shrugged and lowered his voice. 'But if Cassidy is as good as you say he is, he'll be fine.'

'Even he'll struggle against that many.'

'Relax. Luther won't kill him.'

Nat swirled round in the saddle to face Spenser.

'How can you know that?'

'This close to the raid it might cause too many problems. Unless Cassidy's stupid enough to say that he's a lawman, Luther will just rough him up and run him off. Now, hurry up.'

Nat sighed, then hurried his horse to a gallop and sped past Spenser.

'All right,' he shouted over his shoulder. 'But no matter what you say, I ain't proud of myself.'

CHAPTER 6

There were just too many of them.

Every time Cassidy fought to his feet, another man bundled into him and knocked him down again. It'd been long minutes since he'd lost his gun and even longer since he'd last seen Hearst, but he guessed his deputy was faring as badly as he was.

Cassidy threw yet another wild punch at the man before him, but even though he slugged his opponent to the floor, firm arms wrapped around his chest from behind.

Cassidy flexed his back and slammed his feet into a firm stance, then tried to hurl the man over his shoulder, but he couldn't buck his assailant and instead, the man pulled him upright.

And when Cassidy looked up, he faced a row of six men, all of whom glared at him with their eyes bright and their fists raised.

Behind them, two men had thrust both of Hearst's arms way up his back and were holding him upright. Hearst was dishevelled and fierce determination burned in his eyes, but the men holding him were gripping him firmly.

'You got us wrong,' Cassidy said, raising his arms at the elbows. 'We weren't looking for trouble.'

One man raised his fist, ready to pummel Cassidy's exposed stomach, but Luther pushed him aside and swaggered to the front of the row of men.

'But you were looking for someone,' he said. 'And I don't like that.'

'We weren't looking for anybody. We just wanted provisions.'

'I don't believe you. So, tell me. Who are you? Bounty hunters?' Luther spat on the floor. 'Lawmen?'

'Nothing like that.'

Talbot Malloy, a squat and swarthy man, wandered up to Luther and drew him aside, then whispered in his ear.

Luther shook his head and pushed Talbot away.

'We can't take the chance,' he grunted.

'But,' Talbot said, 'these men might not be—'

'Quiet!' Luther roared, raising a fist that forced Talbot to back away a pace. 'I say what we do.'

'You know who gives the orders,' Talbot murmured, then rolled his shoulders and advanced on Luther. 'And that ain't you.'

'And if Fe— he were here, he'd say the same as me.' Luther swung round to face Cassidy and pointed a firm finger at him. 'You men picked the wrong place to buy your provisions.'

'You can't mean to kill us?' Hearst shouted. He struggled against the men holding him, but they'd clasped his arms in a firm grip.

Luther licked his lips, nodding.

'But that'll attract attention,' Talbot said, 'if some-one realizes they're missing.'

Luther shrugged. 'Then don't kill them here. And bury them somewhere where nobody will ever find them.'

Talbot stared at Luther a moment, then nodded and directed the men holding Cassidy and Hearst to head for the door.

Cassidy dug his heels in, so Talbot joined the man holding him and his sharp shove wheeled Cassidy forward. Then the two men's solid grip dragged him over the floor.

'You're making a mistake,' Cassidy shouted. He kicked back, trying to gain purchase on the smooth floor, but the men holding him pushed him towards the door.

'*Not* killing you would be the mistake,' Luther said, grinning.

Cassidy winced then went limp, forcing the men who were holding him to use all their efforts to push him towards the door. But, on their third step, Cassidy slammed his feet to the floor and with his stance firm, hurled his arms out.

His sudden action surprised one of the men and the grip on his right arm lessened as the man fell away.

And, with this encouragement, Cassidy thrust his shoulders down, Talbot's grip being so strong that he lifted Talbot's feet from the floor and hurled him over his shoulder.

Cassidy let Talbot's momentum drag them both down and the two men tumbled to the floor, entan-gled.

As Talbot floundered, Cassidy lunged for Talbot's holster. But even as his fingers brushed the gun stock, Luther leapt at him and kicked his hand away, and within moments, two more men leapt on him, his chance disappearing even as it came.

Cassidy squirmed, but strong hands held him down. From under the tangle of bodies, he peered up at Luther.

'We're just two passers-by,' he shouted. 'Let us go and you'll never see us again.'

Luther snorted. 'Don't worry. *Nobody* will ever see you again. Now, take them outside and no more of this—'

'Wait!' a voice ordered from the doorway.

Cassidy looked to the door to see Sheriff Ballard stride into the post and aim his Peacemaker at Luther's back.

Luther turned on his heel and glared at Ballard, then softened his expression and held his hands wide.

'Sheriff Ballard,' he murmured, 'we don't often see you around these parts.'

'You don't,' Ballard snapped, pacing into the centre of the post. 'But when I got trouble to stop, I go anywhere.'

Luther raised his hands, a benign smile on his face.

'But *we* ain't done nothing wrong.'

Ballard gestured with his gun towards Hearst, then to the heap of men holding Cassidy down.

'And why are you holding these two men?'

Luther glanced at Cassidy and Hearst, then

flinched, almost as if he was noticing their plight for the first time.

'That was just a misunderstanding and we were *dealing* with it.'

Luther clicked his fingers and the men holding Cassidy peeled off him, one by one. Then the men holding Hearst pushed him forward.

'That so?' Ballard said, looking at Cassidy.

'Yeah,' Cassidy said, straightening his ruffled jacket. 'We just had ourselves a misunderstanding.'

'Seems a mighty big misunderstanding to me.'

'Not much,' Luther said. 'These good-for-nothing varmints were . . . were trying to take provisions they hadn't paid for.'

'Stealing, eh? You want to press charges?'

Ballard glanced at the trading post owner who wandered out from behind the counter.

'Nope,' he said. 'They've paid now. So, as long as they don't come here again, I ain't concerned.'

Ballard nodded. 'Then I'll escort them away, if that's all right with you, Luther?'

Luther glanced at Cassidy, then nodded. 'Yeah. That sounds like justice to me.'

Ballard stood aside and pointed to the door.

As Cassidy and Hearst collected their guns, Luther and Talbot flanked the doorway, their arms folded and their gazes lively. But when Cassidy and Hearst slipped outside, they averted their eyes from them.

Ballard stood a moment, then followed them.

Without further word, the three men paced to their horses and mounted them, then headed to the

Bear Creek trail.

'Keep a calm pace,' Ballard said, staring straight ahead.

'But they will come for us,' Cassidy said.

'They won't,' Ballard grunted.

For 200 yards, they rode at a steady pace, but the desire to look back continued to pester Cassidy so, when they reached the trail, he glanced over his shoulder.

Outside the trading post, three men were mounting their horses.

'We got to speed now,' Cassidy said. 'They're coming.'

'They won't.' Ballard glanced at Cassidy from the corner of his eye. 'For once in your miserable existence, believe me.'

Cassidy rode on, expecting to hear approaching hoofbeats pounding after them, but the faint noises he heard were far away, and receding.

With Ballard not initiating conversation, Cassidy and Hearst remained silent, but Cassidy glanced left and right at the low hills, still expecting Luther to mount a raid.

But, after twenty minutes of steady riding, they reached the junction of the eastward trail and the trail to Bear Creek with still no pursuit starting.

'This is where we part company,' Ballard said, pulling his horse to a halt but still peering down the trail towards Bear Creek.

Cassidy glanced east. 'You expect us to head back to Monotony?'

Ballard whistled a steady breath through his

nostrils, his hands clenching the reins in a knuckle-whitening grip.

'Yesterday, I asked you to leave. Today, I'm *ordering* you to go back to Morbid.'

'Monotony,' Cassidy murmured, then raised his voice. 'But you can't order us to leave now. I saw Nathaniel. But he escaped when those men jumped us.'

'And I'm already regretting saving your lives,' Ballard roared, whirling round in the saddle to glare at Cassidy, his eyes blazing.

Cassidy raised his hands. 'I'm obliged to you for saving us, but I don't understand—'

'And that's your problem,' Ballard yelled, spit flying from his mouth. 'You don't understand. You're a man who sees nothing wrong in riding into another lawman's territory and running that lawman's investigations for him. And even when you foul up everything you touch, you ain't concerned.'

'We got into some trouble, but I was getting close to Nathaniel. And he won't have gone far. I know him and his habits and he'll—'

'I don't care about that low-life.'

'You're a lawman. You have to care.'

Ballard turned his horse to face Cassidy and leaned forward in the saddle. For long moments he appraised him, then shook his head, the anger gone from his eyes to leave just tiredness.

'I don't care when I was getting close to Rodrigo Fernandez.'

'If you're close to him, I'll do whatever I can to help.'

'I've had enough of your *help*. It took me a year to find the right man to give me information about Fernandez. It took me six months to set up the right place to catch him. It took me a month to create a situation where I could catch him.'

Cassidy closed his eyes a moment. 'You're talking about Dewey Wade and the trading post?'

'So, you figured that out. But why couldn't you figure out the rest?'

Cassidy glanced away, sighing. 'I reckon I can see it now.'

'And that's too late. I let the petty outlaws who congregated at that trading post know the times I'd visit so that it'd be a safe place for the likes of Rodrigo Fernandez. And sure enough, Fernandez has used that post as one of his meeting places.' Ballard sighed. 'Want to guess who was going to be there tonight?'

Cassidy glanced away from Ballard's firm gaze to look at Hearst, who returned a wince.

'Rodrigo Fernandez,' he whispered.

'Perhaps you're not as stupid as you look.' Ballard gestured all around at the surrounding hills. 'I've got ten deputies hidden along every trail waiting for Fernandez to show. In case he broke through that cordon, I got a backup posse in Bear Creek. But now, Fernandez won't come tonight, or ever. And I have to start all over again.' Ballard slapped his thigh and swirled round to stare straight ahead. 'You just ensured that Rodrigo Fernandez escapes justice for a whole lot longer. You proud of that?'

For long moments Cassidy didn't reply, but when

Ballard turned to look at him with his eyebrows raised, he shook his head.

'I'm not. But I just didn't know.'

'And that sums up your life.' Ballard raised the reins. 'Now, leave before I find a crime to charge you with.'

Cassidy took a deep breath. 'Sheriff Ballard, I was wrong. If it helps, I'm sorry.'

Ballard snorted and shook the reins, hurrying his horse on ahead to leave Cassidy and Hearst alone on the trail.

'It doesn't,' he muttered.

In silence, Cassidy and Hearst rode down the trail away from Bear Creek, neither man daring to look at the other.

Ahead, the trail stretched on.

It was a good day to the county border. But by sundown, they'd only travelled ten miles.

'You want to keep going?' Hearst said. 'Moon's up in an hour.'

'No. We make camp here.'

Cassidy pulled his horse from the trail and headed for a tangle of boulders that would afford them shelter from the low breeze whipping across the plains.

'And tomorrow, we head back to Monotony?'

Cassidy dismounted and stood a moment, staring back down the trail towards Bear Creek, then looked up at Hearst.

'Got no choice. Ballard was right. I did everything wrong back there. My determination to get

Nathaniel ruined his investigation. I can't act in his territory any longer.'

Hearst dismounted. 'That don't sound like you talking.'

Cassidy busied himself with his horse's rigging, but then broke off to turn to Hearst.

'And what do you reckon we should do?'

'I hate leaving when a lawman reckons I'm a fool. So, we should head back to Bear Creek and put things right.'

'How?'

'We capture Rodrigo Fernandez ourselves and earn Ballard's respect.'

Cassidy searched Hearst's eyes, but his deputy fixed him with a firm gaze.

'I appreciate the idea. But we can't put things right with Ballard, other than staying out of his way.'

'I've never thought you'd give up,' Hearst said, tipping back his hat. 'But it seems we *are* leaving.'

'Eventually, we are. But we still have Nathaniel to capture. And when we've done that, we'll leave.'

Hearst closed his eyes a moment. 'You're getting even more confusing, Cassidy. I thought you said we weren't investigating in Ballard's territory any longer.'

'We ain't.'

'But we *are* still leaving?'

'We are.'

'Now, don't say that a good deputy should know what you mean, because I don't understand you right now.' Hearst slapped his thigh. 'How *do* we capture Nathaniel if we ain't investigating?'

For the first time since they had left Ballard, Cassidy let a smile emerge.

'We don't.'

Hearst sighed. 'Cassidy, you're getting stranger and stranger.'

CHAPTER 7

By the edge of a sprawl of spidery cottonwood trees that protected him from casual interest, Nat paced back and forth.

He avoided looking at his horse, which he'd tethered under an overhanging rock, fifty yards back, knowing that he needed all his control to avoid jumping on his steed and galloping back to the trading post.

But the wiser part of him knew that he couldn't do that now – not after running when he had a chance to act.

Then he saw the rider approaching from across the plains. Nat edged back into the trees, but then recognized the man as Spenser and hailed him.

'What happened?' he shouted.

In a cloud of dust, Spenser pulled his horse to a halt and dismounted.

'Sheriff Ballard rode into the post and saved him,' he said. 'Fernandez won't show now.'

Nat closed his eyes a moment. 'Anyone reckon we did anything wrong?'

'Luther reckons Cassidy was after us, and that

we're more trouble than we're worth, but I reckon we're still in Fernandez's set-up. And hopefully, that means Cassidy won't try to get you again.'

Nat sighed. 'Wrong. Cassidy won't avoid trouble.'

Spenser shrugged. 'Then that's his problem.'

'It ain't. I won't do anything to get a friend killed – even an ex-friend.' Nat turned and headed into the cottonwood trees. 'And that means I have no choice.'

'What you mean?' Spenser shouted, but when Nat thrust his head down and continued pacing, he hurried after him. 'I said – what do you mean?'

Twenty yards from his horse, Nat stopped and turned.

'It means I'm giving myself up.'

Spenser snorted a harsh laugh. 'You can't be serious.'

'I am. Cassidy knows how to get to me. And he knew that putting himself in danger was the best way of making me turn myself in.'

Spenser stared at Nat, an incredulous smile on his lips, but when Nat returned his stare, he threw his hands high.

'You can't be saying that he deliberately tried to get himself killed to shame you into giving yourself up.'

'I'm not. Cassidy didn't know Luther would attack him, but he knew I'd know he was in danger.'

Nat turned and headed towards his horse.

'You really are serious about this,' Spenser murmured. 'But what about your promises to me?'

Nat unwound his horse's reins from the tree.

'You'll be fine. The plan probably wouldn't have

worked anyway. Just sell the information you have to Isaac Gillespie or to Sheriff Ballard.' Nat mounted his horse. 'That'll be enough for a good return without putting yourself in danger.'

'I ain't interested. We had a deal.'

'We did.' Nat bunched the reins in his fist. 'But my promises to Cassidy are older.'

Spenser stared up at Nat, then sighed and kicked the earth.

'Nothing I can say will stop you acting like a damn fool. But what about you? You're walking into a jail sentence when you could walk into being a rich man.'

'I'll get five years, maybe seven.' Nat swung his horse round to face the trail. 'But that's a whole lot better than being rich and getting Cassidy killed.'

'I got to hand it to you, Cassidy,' Hearst said. He locked his hands together and sat back against the boulder behind him. 'With every passing hour, you get stranger.'

'How so?' Cassidy said, tossing a spare twig on to their camp-fire.

'I thought we'd head back to Monotony at sun-up, but that was two hours ago, and we're still sitting by the camp-fire.'

'I told you – I'm not returning without Nathaniel.'

'I know. But as far as I can tell, your method of finding him is to sit here and wait for him to ride into our camp.'

Cassidy firmed his jaw, then wafted a hand through the flames.

'And he will.'

Hearst shrugged and leaned forward. 'And that's because you shamed him, or . . . or something?'

'Or something.'

'All right. I accept you don't want to talk about it.' Hearst licked his lips and shuffled on to his haunches. 'But as you're a betting man, do you want to bet on this?'

'This is no betting matter,' Cassidy snapped, swirling round to glare at Hearst. Then he lowered his head and softened his voice. 'I'm sorry.'

'Forget it.' Hearst sat. 'I know this means a lot to you.'

Cassidy peered through the fire at the plains beyond, then snorted.

'Perhaps I should lighten up,' he murmured, then turned to Hearst. 'So, if Nathaniel rides into our camp, you'll stand me a night's drinks.'

'Deal,' Hearst said, smiling.

'And if he rides into camp within a time of my choosing, you'll stand me a week's drinks.'

Hearst grinned. 'Even better – what's your time limit?'

'Within the next . . .' – Cassidy rocked his head from side to side – 'two minutes.'

'Two . . .' Hearst swirled round to peer in the direction Cassidy had been looking.

From across the plains, a man was riding towards them, his gait slow.

'You still want to take that bet?' Cassidy asked.

Hearst tipped back his hat. 'If this is him, I'll pay up, gladly.'

The man maintained his steady pacing until his horse stood on the edge of the campsite, then dismounted and faced Cassidy.

'Cassidy,' he said.

'Nathaniel,' Cassidy said, standing.

'I answer to Nat now.'

'You used to answer to your given name, *Nathaniel.*'

'I used to do plenty of things.' Nat flashed a smile. 'But why do you want me?'

'A Wanted poster says you've committed crimes.'

'That means nothing.'

'I know that.' Cassidy kicked a branch into the fire. 'But it ain't my job to decide whether you did wrong or not.'

'It ain't as simple as right and wrong.' Nat shrugged. 'I just pushed the rules too far.'

'You didn't push the rules,' Cassidy snapped, 'you broke them.'

'I was trying to survive. And as a bounty hunter, that ain't easy.'

'Then you should have stayed a lawman. The rules are more obvious.'

'I made my choices,' Nat said, then sighed and lowered his head. 'But you need to know that you weren't to blame for anything I've done.'

'I already knew that.'

Nat raised his head. 'I just assumed that was why you were here.'

'Then you assumed wrong.'

'And,' Hearst said, rolling to his feet, 'you'll remove your gunbelt.'

Nat glanced at Hearst, then turned his gaze back on Cassidy.

'I'm not doing that because you aren't arresting me.' Nat raised his hands to chest level with the palms facing Cassidy. 'But I am turning myself in to you. And I give my word that I won't run.'

'You ain't dictating anything to—'

'Enough, Hearst,' Cassidy said. He kicked a heap of dust over the fire and pointed to Nat's horse. 'Nathaniel has given his word. And we got a long journey ahead of us.'

CHAPTER 8

At a canter, the three riders headed east along the trail. Cassidy led, Nat was in the middle, and the still sceptical Hearst brought up the rear.

Faced with a four-day journey back to Monotony, Cassidy dreaded the lengthy taut silences that he expected would fill the days ahead, although these were more preferable than having to talk to his old friend.

Sure enough, for three hours they rode in total silence using a steady, mile-eating pace. But when the sun was at its highest and they were heading through an outcropping of cottonwoods beside a rounded hillock, the first rider they'd seen today headed down the slope towards them.

Cassidy watched the rider approach, seeing nothing in his steady gait to suggest he was trouble, but when the rider was fifty yards away, he turned in the saddle to check that Hearst was also alert.

Hearst *was* watching the rider, but Nat was sitting firm in the saddle, his gaze boring into the newcomer.

Cassidy swirled round, but it was to see the approaching rider rip his gun from its holster and aim it down at him.

'Stop right there,' the rider shouted, pulling his horse to a halt.

'Do nothing hasty,' Cassidy said, raising his hands. 'We're just—'

'Spenser,' Nat shouted, 'what are you doing?'

The rider, Spenser, shrugged. 'I'm here to free you.'

Cassidy glanced at Nat. 'Is this your partner?'

'Yeah,' Nat said. 'And he ain't trouble.'

'Nathaniel, he has a gun on me.'

'And he'll put it down when he knows you won't arrest him.'

For long moments Cassidy glared at Nat, then rolled his shoulders.

'You ain't ordering me. So, if that's the way you want—'

'Be quiet,' Spenser roared. 'Nobody is arresting anyone. I'm just here to save Nat from himself.'

'Obliged for the thought,' Nat said. 'But I made my decision last night.'

'And there's more at stake here than just your pride.'

'There isn't.' Nat glared hard at Spenser, then glanced at Cassidy. 'I'll speak . . . Can I speak to him, in private?'

Cassidy shook his head. 'You don't get this, Nathaniel, do you? I'm taking you in. And you aren't giving me orders.'

'And I'm not. I promised I'd come quietly. And I

will. Let me prove that you can trust me.'

Cassidy glanced over Nat's shoulder at Hearst, who returned a bemused shake of the head. But Cassidy still nodded.

As Nat dismounted, Hearst glared at Cassidy, but Cassidy leaned forward in the saddle, watching Spenser dismount.

The two men sauntered away from them and stopped beside an outlying tree where, with much gesticulating, they argued, but about exactly what, Cassidy couldn't hear.

'Cassidy,' Hearst said. He drew his horse alongside him and tipped back his hat. 'We got two wanted men, both armed, and we're letting them discuss whether or not they want to be arrested. This ain't any version of the law I understand.'

'It ain't. But trust me.' Cassidy flashed Hearst an encouraging smile. 'Sometimes, you do what you have to do to keep the peace.'

As Hearst shook his head, Nat turned from Spenser, but Spenser grabbed his arm and pulled him back and the two men faced each other, repeatedly waggling fingers in each other's faces and grunting demands at each other.

But, by degrees, the gesticulating and arguing lessened and, with a last pat on the back from Spenser, Nat turned and strode back to Cassidy.

'I've agreed with Spenser,' he said, 'that I'll ask you a question.'

'Save yourself the trouble,' Cassidy said. 'I ain't offering you and Spenser any deals.'

'And I ain't looking for one. I'll tell you what we're

doing, and whatever you decide, I'll still hand myself in.'

'And Spenser?'

'He'll take his chances, but being as he has a drawn gun, I guess you'll have to track him down in the usual way.'

Cassidy glanced at Spenser, confirming he still had his gun drawn, but he was resting it in the crook of his elbow.

'All right. Tell me what you're doing.'

'We're bringing in Rodrigo Fernandez.'

Cassidy snorted. 'I'm sorry, Nathaniel. I don't believe that. You're part of his gang.'

'We *were* in the trading post with other members of Fernandez's gang. But that's how we work. We infiltrate, gain contacts, gather inside information.'

'And then you capture outlaws and collect the bounty?'

'Yep.'

Cassidy leaned forward, a hand on his hip and his gaze searching Nat's eyes.

'And sometimes, you keep the outlaws' loot for yourselves?'

'Sometimes we do that, too.'

'And sometimes, you steal the loot before the outlaws get their hands on it?'

Nat's eyes flickered with a hint of something, perhaps doubt, perhaps shame, before he blinked it away.

'I can't explain to you what we do. But I guess we look for . . . for *opportunities.*'

'And what are you looking for here?'

'Only what I've said. Let us bring in Rodrigo Fernandez.'

'Letting you and Spenser talk has pushed my principles to the maximum. And I can't let two wanted men go free even if it is to catch another wanted man.'

'But I'm one of those men. And I'll come quietly afterwards.'

Cassidy glanced at the surrounding low hills, sighing.

'I want to trust you,' he murmured. 'So, prove that you ain't seeking one of your opportunities and I will.'

'I got no proof, but if I help bring Rodrigo Fernandez to justice, I guess that might reduce my sentence.'

'It might. But you used to bring outlaws to justice because it was your job, not to reduce your sentence.'

'Those days are long gone. But does it matter if I bring in Fernandez?'

Cassidy stared at Nat, seeing in his earnest gaze that desire to do right that he'd seen in him the first time they'd met.

But he still shook his head.

'It *does* matter. And once, you'd have known that it wasn't worth asking me that.'

Nat lowered his head and when he raised it his eyes were blank, but he still nodded then paced towards his horse.

'Hey,' Spenser shouted. 'You can't walk away from me.'

Nat turned. 'I did what I asked. I made my offer.

And Cassidy refused it. The matter is closed.'

'It ain't to me.' Spenser thrust his gun in its holster and stormed two long paces towards Nat.

Nat shook his head and moved to mount his horse, but Spenser pounded across the ground and slammed a hand on his shoulder, halting him.

Nat shrugged the hand off, but Spenser grabbed his arm and pulled him round to face him.

'And how will you stop me?' Nat muttered.

Spenser glared at Nat, then glanced away, but he swirled back and with a short-armed jab, hammered his jaw.

Nat shrugged off the blow and ripped a round-armed slug into Spenser's guts.

Spenser snorted, then hurled himself at Nat. He grabbed him in a firm neck hold and bent him double, then tried to pull him to the ground.

On his horse, Cassidy glanced at Hearst, who had already drawn his gun and trained it down at the fighting twosome, but he glanced at Cassidy and provided a bemused smile. Cassidy drew his gun, too, and peered down at the fight, but Nat and Spenser appeared to have forgotten about their audience as they slugged out their differences.

Nat set his feet into a wide and firm stance then threw out his arms, hurling Spenser away from him. Spenser stumbled back a pace and Nat wrapped his arms around Spenser's midriff then, with his arms bunched, tried to wrestle him to the ground.

Spenser resisted, wrapping an arm around Nat's chest, and the two men circled on the spot, wriggling as each man tried to pull the other man down. But neither Spenser nor Nat could drag the other man to the ground and they rocked back and forth.

Then Spenser's foot slipped and, taking advantage of him being momentarily off-balance, Nat kicked his legs from under him. As Spenser still had a grip of Nat's chest, the two men tumbled to the ground. But Nat twisted out from Spenser's grip and with both hands, pinned his shoulders to the dirt. Spenser squirmed, trying to buck Nat, but with all Nat's weight bearing down on him, he failed to move him, and he lay back.

'You're wrong,' he muttered. 'Join me.'

'I ain't,' Nat snapped.

Cassidy coughed and favoured them with a wide smile.

'If you two gentlemen have finished *discussing* what you want to do,' he said. His high, false voice dragged a chuckle from Hearst. 'I'd be most obliged if you'd let me tell you what you'll do.'

Nat and Spenser flinched, Cassidy's taunt apparently dragging them back to the realization that two lawmen were watching them.

Nat released his hold of Spenser's shoulders and raised a hand.

'*We* are not joining you,' he said. 'I am, but Spenser isn't.'

'Nathaniel,' Cassidy snapped, 'I promise you that I'll treat you both fairly. And I'll tell the court that you came peacefully and of your own choosing. But letting an outlaw go free because you want me to is too much.'

Nat sneered. 'I will come with you, but Spenser goes free. That's the deal, or you'll face the longest four days of your life trying to keep me in line.'

'Don't threaten me, Nathaniel.'

'He ain't,' a voice shouted from beside the trees, 'but I am.'

Cassidy swirled round to see Dewey Wade step out from behind a tree with a gun drawn and aimed at him.

'You?' Cassidy said, failing to keep the laughter from his voice.

'Yeah,' Dewey said, 'me.'

'You couldn't shoot your own foot off.'

'When I've had as many drinks as I'd had when you last saw me, you're right.' Dewey raised his left hand and held it flat, showing Cassidy that it was still. 'But I'm cold sober, right now, and unless you step away from Spenser and Nat, you'll be cold dead.'

'Dewey, quit trying to be an outlaw and put down that gun.'

'I can't. Even I can better myself. And Spenser has convinced me that bringin' in Fernandez will do that. So, I'm holdin' this gun on you until you release your prisoners and we can go after him.'

Cassidy glanced at Nat and Spenser, then at Dewey. He chuckled a harsh laugh and raised his hands.

'I guess we're going after Fernandez.'

'Cassidy,' Hearst muttered.

Cassidy raised a hand and turned to his deputy.

'Hearst, a saloon bum is holding us at gunpoint

demanding that we let him and two outlaws capture another outlaw.' Cassidy smiled. 'So, I reckon it's time to bow to the absurdity of it all.'

CHAPTER 9

Two miles down the Bear Creek trail, Spenser pulled his horse to a halt and peered over his shoulder.

'Cassidy ain't following us,' he said.

'I know,' Nat grunted. 'He gave his word.'

As Spenser rolled his shoulders and faced the trail ahead, Dewey punched the air.

'I did good,' he said, 'didn't I?'

'Yeah,' Spenser said. 'You did good.'

'That mean you'll let me in on everythin' now?'

'On everything,' Spenser said, then turned to Nat, who was still staring ahead, his jaw set firm. 'Sorry I had to hit you, Nat.'

Nat rubbed his chin, the first hint of a smile invading his lips since he'd left Cassidy.

'I reckon I won that fight.'

'Perhaps, but I don't understand you. You claim you'll never go back on your word.'

'And I won't.'

'But you got no choice now. You promised Cassidy that you'd bring in Rodrigo Fernandez, except we ain't doing that.'

'We *are* doing that.'

74

'In a way we are, but that don't exactly explain our plans. You avoided lying by not mentioning some vital details.'

For a full minute Nat rode on, then turned in the saddle to Spenser.

'And what of it?'

'Well, either you'll break your word to me, or you'll break your word to Cassidy.'

'I don't aim to do either.'

'How?'

Nat sighed. 'When I work that out, I'll let you know.'

'We can't trust Nathaniel, surely?' Hearst said.

'We can,' Cassidy said. 'He gave me his word.'

Hearst pulled his horse to a halt and leaned forward in the saddle, waiting until Cassidy turned on the trail and headed back to him.

'So you said. But that was when we had him under arrest. But now that he's headed off with Spenser on a mission to catch Fernandez, you can't know for sure that we'll ever see him again.'

'We will – have no doubt.'

For long moments Hearst stared at Cassidy, then provided a reluctant nod.

'All right, but I still don't like this.'

'Neither do I.' Cassidy shrugged. 'But why have you changed? Yesterday, you were all fired up to catch Fernandez and reclaim our dignity.'

'I was, but I guess I don't like who I'm working with now.'

'You're working with me.'

Hearst looked at Cassidy, then shrugged and shook the reins, hurrying his horse past him and back to their campsite.

'Ah, our bounty hunters,' Isaac Gillespie said, leaning back behind his desk in Bear Creek's bank.

Nat and Spenser swung to a halt before the desk.

'We want more information about this gold shipment,' Nat said.

'I gave you all the details.'

'But this time, we want to know the details that you didn't tell us,' Spenser said, as he paced to Nat's side. He raised his eyebrows. 'Such as the name of the potential weak link in your system.'

'There is no weak link.'

'There always is. Somebody always passes information on to the wrong people.' Spenser slapped his hands flat to Isaac's desk and smiled. 'So, who do you suspect?'

Isaac met Spenser's gaze. 'Nobody. I trust them all.'

'Everybody has a price – even you.'

'I don't.'

Spenser snorted. 'You talked to us for five hundred dollars.'

'I didn't,' Isaac murmured with a gulp. 'That was the bank's money.'

'It was. And in return, you told us plenty.' Spenser pushed himself up from the desk and stood with his arms folded. 'We could have raised that money elsewhere and paid our way into your favour.'

Isaac glanced down. 'You didn't, did you?'

As Spenser chuckled, Nat glared long and hard at Isaac, then tipped back his hat and smiled.

'We didn't,' he said. He watched Isaac sigh with relief. 'But Spenser was making a point. Everybody has their price, *everybody*. So, tell us – who do you suspect to be the weak link in your delivery system?'

Isaac rubbed his chin, then drummed his fingers on his desk, his eyes downcast.

'I guess if you put it like that. . . .'

CHAPTER 10

'When do you reckon this raid will happen?' Hearst asked.

Cassidy shrugged and rested his crossed feet on the seat before him.

'Patience, Hearst. It'll come soon enough.'

It was the day after they'd released Nat, and to Nat's instructions, they'd travelled back to Lincoln and boarded the train to Denver.

Isaac Gillespie had claimed that the gold shipment had been loaded on to this train at Beaver Ridge, and that it would now be in the transportation carriage. At some stage, known only to Isaac and a few others, the train would make an unscheduled stop and the gold would embark on its journey to Bear Creek.

And it was then that Fernandez was most likely to raid.

So, Cassidy and Hearst had seated themselves in the passenger carriage directly behind the transportation carriage.

With five men available, two on the train, and

three off it, plus the shipment guards with the gold, Cassidy reckoned they had the resources to bring Fernandez to justice – even if one of the men on his side was Dewey Wade.

But, after six hours of waiting, neither the unscheduled stop nor Fernandez's raid had materialized.

'I ain't seen as many guards as I thought I'd see,' Hearst said.

'Nathaniel said that the set-up might be unusual. Twelve heavily armed guards didn't keep the last shipment from Fernandez's clutches. He reckoned they might try a different approach this time.'

'Either way, I can't tell if any of the people on this train are disguised guards. Nor can I tell if any are in Fernandez's gang.'

Cassidy shuffled down in his seat and used the movement to glance around the carriage.

Two seats back, a man was cleaning his fingernails with a knife. Opposite him, a man had dismantled his gun and was cleaning each part with the studied concentration of a man whose life depended on his weapon always being ready.

'Some of these men look shifty-eyed,' Cassidy said.

'And that's the problem,' Hearst said. 'They all look shifty-eyed to me.'

Hearst cocked his head, signifying that Cassidy should look at the man sitting in the seat that was level with them. This man was repeatedly flicking his gaze towards the door at the front of the carriage while drumming his fingers on his leg.

Cassidy sighed and leaned back to avoid this man noticing that they were looking at him, but Hearst stood and sauntered to the man's side.

Hearst leaned towards the train window to look outside and, as the man shuffled back and peered at him from under a lowered hat, he glanced down and tipped his hat, then returned to sit beside Cassidy.

'Recognize him?' Cassidy whispered, leaning to Hearst.

'Nope,' Hearst whispered. 'But he's in on the raid.'

'How could you tell?'

'I just could.'

'Seems you're getting those instincts that'll make you a sheriff one . . .' Cassidy nudged Hearst, but Hearst was already staring straight ahead.

The blue-uniformed conductor had left the transportation carriage, then leaned back on the wall and planted his feet wide to counteract the swaying of the train.

The conductor flicked his gaze down the carriage and rubbed his nose.

Then the man to their side stood and sauntered down the carriage. He tipped his hat to the conductor, then shook his hand, but within the gesture, Cassidy saw money change hands before the man walked through the door.

The conductor glanced around the carriage, his gaze darting between the passengers, then followed the man through.

'What you reckon to that?' Hearst asked.

'Same as you – that man is in Fernandez's gang and a bribe just changed hands.'

'You don't sound surprised.'

'Nathaniel was right about the presence of a weak link. For a raid to work, you need inside information, and that conductor is helping Rodrigo Fernandez.'

'So,' Hearst said, tipping back his hat, 'you reckon that the raid will come soon?'

'That's my guess.'

'When are we acting?'

From ahead, a gunshot sounded, the sound muffled, but loud enough to make several passengers behind them shuffle on their seats and peer through the windows.

Cassidy turned to Hearst. 'Now would seem like the right time.'

Cassidy rolled to his feet and, with Hearst at his heels, pounded down the carriage for the front door. He threw open the door and hurtled through.

Neither the conductor nor the man who had followed him through was there, so he vaulted the gap between the carriages to stand outside the transportation carriage. When Hearst joined him, he kicked open the door.

Side by side, they burst in.

Inside, four unarmed men sat around an upturned barrel set before a huge crate, a poker game in progress.

But, by the opened double-doors at the side of the carriage, the conductor had a Peacemaker aimed at the group.

Cassidy shouted a warning to the poker players as he dashed three long paces and leapt at the conductor, who merely stared at Cassidy, transfixed. Cassidy grabbed the conductor's gun hand and pushed the gun high. On the edge of the door, both men flexed back and forth.

The poker players muttered something, but a barked command from Hearst silenced them.

Then Cassidy dashed the conductor's gun hand against the side of the carriage, ripping the gun from his grip and, as his opponent floundered, Cassidy slugged his jaw, knocking him back a pace.

The conductor stumbled into the doorframe and hung on a moment, but the wind whipped by and tore his grip away. He wheeled his arms, fighting for balance, but then tumbled from the carriage to land out of sight.

Cassidy swirled round to face the poker players.

'Any other trouble yet?' he shouted.

'Only person lookin' for trouble is you,' a round-shouldered old-timer said, raising his hands high. 'But we ain't opposin' you.'

'I ain't trouble. I'm Sheriff Cassidy Yates and this is Deputy Frank Hearst. And you?'

'Art, Art Weston.'

'So, Art, Art Weston, what happened to the man who came in here?'

Weston nodded down the length of the carriage.

'He's down there somewhere, searchin' for some-thin'.'

'And you let him?'

'He's searchin' for his own property.'

'And you didn't think he might be after the gold shipment.'

'What gold shipment?'

Cassidy pointed to the huge crate behind Weston,

the only crate large enough to contain the gold.

'I mean *that* gold.'

Weston glanced over the shoulder at the crate, his brow furrowed, then turned back to Cassidy, shaking his head.

'That crate just has a heap of old animal furs in it and God knows what else.'

Cassidy sniffed, but the wind whipping in from the open doorway kept any odours at bay. He strode closer to Weston and, on the third pace, the stench of long dead animals invaded his nostrils.

He glanced at Hearst, who strode to the crate, but when he reached it, he turned away, wafting his hand before his wrinkled nose.

'That ain't no gold, Cassidy,' he said.

'Like we told you,' Weston said, slapping his cards on the crate.

'Then why was the conductor holding you at gunpoint?'

'He wasn't holdin' nobody at gunpoint. He'd lost his money and was shootin' at a passing bird.'

'You don't expect me to believe . . .'

The man who they'd followed through the door edged back down the carriage, a leather valise under his arm, but on seeing Cassidy, he dropped the valise and raised his hands high.

'I ain't got nothing to steal,' he shrieked.

Cassidy glanced at the valise, seeing that it was too slim to contain anything valuable. Then he glanced at Hearst, who winced.

'I think we do have to believe Weston,' Hearst said. 'There ain't no gold shipment on this train.'

Cassidy lowered his head, wincing. 'And neither is there any trouble.'

'That is,' Weston said, 'until you arrived.'

CHAPTER 11

'What you reckon?' Cassidy murmured.

Hearst stretched back on his bunk. 'I reckon we're in a whole heap of trouble.'

Cassidy tapped the lowest cell bar with the toe of his boot and sighed.

'That's the biggest understatement I've ever heard.'

The journey back to Bear Creek had been a slow and embarrassing one. Two of the poker players had escorted Cassidy and Hearst, then filed charges for assault with Deputy Cartwright before leaving.

And, for a long night, Cassidy and Hearst had lain in adjoining cells, each lost in their own dark thoughts. Even sun-up and breakfast hadn't lightened the spirits of either man.

'What story are we giving?' Hearst asked.

'The truth.'

'Even about Nathaniel and Spenser?'

'If we have to.'

Hearst sat up on his bunk. 'And what *is* the truth about them?'

Cassidy lowered his head and ran his foot along the cell bar, then turned to Hearst with his hands held wide.

'They had information and we acted on it, but it was inaccurate.'

Hearst snorted. 'Inaccurate is an odd word to describe a lie.'

'Nathaniel didn't lie.'

'He said the gold shipment was on that train, and it wasn't.'

'Perhaps the train was a decoy. Perhaps the bank guards unloaded the shipment before we boarded the train because they learnt that Fernandez would raid it. Perhaps . . .' Cassidy slapped the bars. 'I don't know, but whatever the reason, Nathaniel didn't lie. Somebody lied to him.'

'Stop excusing Nathaniel. He double-crossed us, then ran like the lousy outlaw he is.'

'He didn't. Nathaniel gave me his word.'

Hearst rolled from his bunk and paced across his cell to face Cassidy through the bars.

'I never thought I'd say this, but you made a mistake, Cassidy. You trusted the word of an outlaw.'

'He was my deputy.' Cassidy looked up and fixed Hearst with a firm stare. 'And I trust the word of my deputies.'

'Then trust the word of your current deputy. Nathaniel McBain double-crossed us and now we're in a jail cell instead of him. The sooner you see that, the sooner we can put this right.'

'You're entitled to your opinion, but when you doubt Nathaniel, you doubt me.'

Hearst stared at Cassidy but as Cassidy widened his eyes, he looked away, then sat on his bunk with his hands clenched before him.

'I'm sorry. I don't doubt you,' he murmured, his eyes downcast. 'I guess I'm dreading being on the receiving end of a court's justice.'

'I can live with that.' Cassidy nodded to the window, where the bulky outline of Sheriff Ballard was wandering past. 'But I reckon this part will be the worst.'

As Hearst looked up and winced, Ballard came in and, with his eyes averted from the cells, talked with Deputy Cartwright. Then he pottered around the office, doing anything but approach the cells.

But just as his silence was grinding on Cassidy's nerves, he stalked across the office and peered at him through the bars.

Ballard raised his eyebrows, his gaze blank.

Cassidy returned the stare, content to let the silence irritate Ballard in the same way that it had irritated him.

Ballard snorted. 'So, you got nothing to say for yourself.'

'I made a mistake.'

'Is that an apology?'

'I've done nothing to apologize for, other than to try and catch Rodrigo Fernandez.'

'You're after *him* now!' Ballard hurled his hands above his head. 'Is there no end to your desire to run my town?'

Cassidy closed his eyes and took long, deep breaths.

'Ballard, I wasn't doing that.'

'I know. You couldn't run a wild mustang out of a broken corral.'

'Quit insulting me and see this from my viewpoint.'

'I can't because I don't understand men like you.' Ballard sighed and shook his head. 'First, you tell me how to run my town. Then, you ruin my plan to catch Rodrigo Fernandez. But even that wasn't good enough for you; you then assaulted innocent people.'

'Like I said, I thought Fernandez was raiding the gold shipment on the train.'

'But there was no gold on the train.'

'I know that now. But then I thought—'

'Enough!' Ballard turned, waving his hand in a dismissive gesture at Cassidy. 'I got plenty to do and I don't want to hear your pathetic whining.'

'I heard gunfire,' Cassidy shouted, dashing to the front of the cell. 'What was I suppose to do?'

Ballard swirled round, his eyes blazing. 'You really want an answer?'

Cassidy jutted his jaw, nodding. 'I do want to know what you'd have done.'

Ballard paced to the cell and threw both hands up to grab the bars on either side of Cassidy's head.

'It's simple. If you'd have left like I told you to, you wouldn't have heard no gunfire, and a conductor wouldn't have had a broken arm from you throwing him from a moving train.'

'I guess if that's the way you see it, nothing I can say will help.' Cassidy backed away a pace. 'So, what will you do with us?'

Ballard pulled his hands from the bars to rub his chin, then sneered.

'As you're determined to run my town, what do *you* reckon I should do with you?'

Cassidy searched Ballard's eyes for sarcasm, but on seeing only contempt, he cocked his head to one side and folded his arms.

'Accept that we made a mistake. Then let us leave.'

Ballard glanced over his shoulder at Deputy Cartwright and winked, but he kept his head in a position where Cassidy could see the gesture.

'I *will* let you leave, but not for your reason. Bringing charges against a lawman, even one as worthless as you, is bad for the reputation of all lawmen.'

Cassidy gritted his teeth. 'Obliged.'

Ballard flashed a harsh smile. 'But only after you've apologized.'

'I said I made a mistake.'

'I don't want excuses.' Ballard licked his lips. 'I want a proper, abject apology.'

Cassidy set his feet apart and held his hands, palms up.

'I'm sorry.'

'That ain't enough. Tell me what a worthless lawman you are. Tell me how you discredit the badge every day you wear it.'

'I can't say that because it ain't true.'

Ballard looked Cassidy up and down and sneered. 'Then you'll rot in that cell until you do say it.' He turned on his heel and joined his deputy in animated conversation.

'Cassidy,' Hearst hissed from the adjoining cell, 'we had a chance to leave.'

'We did,' Cassidy said, pacing to the back of the cell. 'But we ain't now.'

'Just say whatever Ballard needs to hear. The words don't matter as much as capturing Nathaniel and Spenser.'

'They do.' Cassidy folded his arms. 'I won't say those words.'

For long moments Hearst glared at Cassidy, then jumped to his feet and dashed to the front of his cell.

'Hey, Sheriff Ballard,' he shouted, slapping the bars.

'What you want?' Ballard asked, looking up.

'Does Cassidy need to apologize for me, too?'

'He does.' Ballard sauntered to the cells and considered Hearst. 'But what are you offering?'

'What do *I* have to say to leave?'

'Nothing you can say will free Cassidy.'

'I ain't asking you to free Cassidy. What do I have to say for *me* to leave.'

'That you apologize,' Ballard said, his eyes gleaming. 'And that you're a worthless lawman.'

'I apologize. I made a mistake.' Hearst glanced over his shoulder at Cassidy, who winced, then stood tall. 'And that makes me a worthless lawman.'

'Hearst!' Cassidy shouted. 'Don't give in to him.'

Ballard raised a hand, a smile ripping out.

'Listen to your deputy, Cassidy. There's hope for him. Now, Hearst, tell me you're a discredit to the badge.'

Hearst looked Ballard straight in the eye. 'I'm a

90

discredit to the badge.'

'Then you can go.' Ballard gestured for Deputy Cartwright to throw him the keys, then unlocked Hearst's cell.

Hearst tipped his hat, then edged through the door. He glanced at Cassidy, but Cassidy returned a slow shake of his head.

Without another word or glance at his boss, Hearst collected his gunbelt then headed outside.

Ballard smiled and turned back to Cassidy with his eyebrows raised.

'Your deputy followed orders even when they were bad orders,' he said. 'But afterwards, he acknowledged his mistake and faced up to it. I understand him.'

'But I don't understand you. No lawman should want to belittle another lawman.'

'But you ain't a real lawman. You're a discredit to the badge.'

Ballard turned away and paced across the office to talk with his deputy. The two men muttered to each other, their voices too low for Cassidy to hear what they discussed. Then they shared a laugh.

With a sly smile emerging, Ballard turned and paced to Cassidy's cell. He unlocked the door, then turned his back on Cassidy and sauntered to his desk.

Cassidy pushed himself away from the back wall.

'Obliged for your change of mind,' he said.

Ballard sat behind his desk and shook his head.

'I've changed nothing. You'll stay there until you say the words.'

'What you mean?' Cassidy pointed at the open cell

door. 'You've unlocked my cell.'

'I did, and if you leave, I'll have every man in the county after you.'

'Ballard, this is too much.'

'Your choice, Cassidy. Tell me what I want to hear and you can go.' Ballard watched the cell door slowly creak open to its full extent then swing back.

'Go to hell,' Cassidy grunted.

'I'm going nowhere.' Ballard chuckled. 'And neither are you for a long, long time.'

CHAPTER 12

'I'm sorry,' the guard said, 'but he wouldn't listen.'

Isaac Gillespie looked up from his desk to face the rapidly advancing Deputy Hearst, the guard trailing behind him.

'Then make him listen or throw him out,' he snapped. 'I've had enough of people barging in here.'

The guard slammed a hand on Hearst's shoulder, but Hearst shrugged it off.

'You *will* see me,' he muttered.

The guard grabbed a firmer grip of Hearst's shoulder.

'And Mr Gillespie is busy.'

Hearst slapped the hand away, but the guard grabbed Hearst's hand and wrenched it back, forcing Hearst to swirl round. He flexed his arm, then pulled both their hands down. But the guard halted Hearst's progress and, with their eyes locked, the two men strained for supremacy.

'It'll only take a minute,' Hearst grunted, 'and that—'

'You heard Mr Gillespie. You're leaving.'

'Wait!' Isaac said, with a resigned sigh. 'If he's quick, I'll listen.'

Hearst and the guard exchanged a long stare. Then, with a snap of the wrist, the guard released Hearst's hand and pushed him a pace towards the desk.

'Go on, then,' he muttered, 'you got one minute.'

'In private,' Hearst said, smiling.

The guard grunted an oath, but Isaac pointed to the door and, with an irritated groan, the guard paced outside.

'So,' Isaac said when the guard had shut the door, 'why have you forced your way in here?'

Hearst sauntered across the office to stand before Isaac's desk.

'We have a problem.'

'Do *we*?'

Hearst slammed both hands down on the desk and glared deep into Isaac's eyes.

'I'm looking for two men, and you know where they are.'

'Names?'

'They probably didn't give their real names, but they claim they're hunting Rodrigo Fernandez, and you've given them information.'

'Sounds like nobody I know.'

'I'm a lawman.'

'Then show me papers that say you got a right to see them.'

Hearst raised an eyebrow and sighed. 'I don't need papers for these men.'

Isaac licked his lips and busied himself with moving papers from one side of his desk to the other.

'Then I can't help you.'

'These men aren't in trouble. They're bounty hunters, and they have . . . have information on some other people I'm looking for.'

Isaac snorted a laugh. 'And I guess these other people don't have names either.'

'They don't.'

Isaac glanced down at the papers coating his desk, then waved in a dismissive manner towards the door.

'I can't help, and I am busy.'

'I know. A gold shipment is coming in to Bear Creek today and you're hoping that Rodrigo Fernandez doesn't raid it.'

Isaac winced. 'Just how many people know about this *secret* shipment?'

'Enough. And once you've told me where I can find them, I'll leave and head after them.'

'I can tell you nothing.'

'Then, I'll go to the saloon.' Hearst turned and strode to the door, but then stomped to a halt. 'Hope I don't get too talkative about what I know.'

Isaac took a long breath, then sighed.

'You want to know about two bounty hunters, you say?'

Hearst turned and smiled.

On hands and knees, Hearst crested the ridge and peered over the other side.

Fifty feet below, two men were kneeling behind a rock, halfway down the slope, peering down at the trail to Bear Creek.

With his eyes narrowed, Hearst confirmed that

95

these men *were* Nat and Spenser – just as Isaac Gillespie had promised.

For five minutes Hearst watched them, confirming that they weren't feigning indifference to his presence. But the men knelt with the easy calm of men who expected to surprise others with their sudden appearance, and didn't expect others to surprise them.

So, with his head down, Hearst paced down the side of the slope. He chose his foot placements with care to avoid dislodging stones, but kept his gun drawn and trained on the men's backs in case they should hear his footfalls.

But such was Nat and Spenser's interest in the trail below that Hearst paced to within twenty yards of them before Nat flinched and swirled round, but it was only to peer down the barrel of Hearst's gun.

'Reach, you two,' Hearst snapped, then glanced around. 'And where's Dewey Wade?'

Nat, then Spenser stood tall and raised their hands to shoulder level.

'In the saloon, I guess,' Nat said. 'But, Deputy Hearst, you got no reason to hold us at gunpoint. We're just—'

'Be quiet.' Hearst paced down the last of the slope to stand before Nat. 'You ain't talking me into releasing you like you talked Cassidy round.'

'We had a deal.'

'And that deal ended the moment you double-crossed us.'

'We didn't do no—'

'Enough! Cassidy is in jail back in Bear Creek because of you.'

Nat blinked hard. 'In jail, why?'

'He believed your lies that Fernandez would raid the train.' Hearst shrugged. 'And, by mistake, he attacked some innocent people.'

'That ain't our fault.'

'It is when you lied about the gold shipment being on the train.'

'The gold *was* on the train to Denver.'

'It wasn't. And now, I'm escorting you to Bear Creek where you'll explain your involvement to Sheriff Ballard.'

Spenser snorted. 'I ain't doing that.'

Hearst appraised Spenser, then smiled and glared at Nat.

'And you, Nathaniel?'

'I'm not doing that now,' Nat said.

'You got no choice.' Hearst firmed his gun hand, but Nat shook his head.

'You didn't listen. I won't do that *now*, but I will do that when we have Fernandez.'

Hearst sneered. 'Cassidy is so convinced you're a decent man that he can't see who you really are. But I'm not Cassidy and I don't believe you're trying to capture Rodrigo Fernandez.'

Nat pointed at the trail below. 'Then why else are we sitting out here, watching the trail?'

'I don't know. For all I know you're planning to raid the gold shipment yourself.'

Hearst searched Nat's eyes for a flicker of concern. He saw none, but Spenser shuffled from foot to foot.

'You got us wrong,' Spenser murmured.

'Perhaps I have or perhaps I haven't, but either

way, the court can decide.' Hearst gestured to Nat and Spenser's horses.

Both Nat and Spenser glanced at them, but then flinched and stared over Hearst's right shoulder.

'We can't leave,' Nat murmured, his gaze set on the top of the ridge. 'We got trouble.'

'I won't fail for that trick,' Hearst said with a snort. 'There ain't no—'

A gunshot blasted, ripping into the earth six inches from Hearst's right foot.

Hearst swirled round to see that a row of men had stood up from behind the rocks at the top of the ridge. He ran his gaze along them, counting fifteen, then sighted the nearest man down the barrel of his gun.

But the man at the end, Luther, swung his gun round and fired at him, the shot initiating a sustained burst of gunfire that blasted around Hearst, ripping dirt into his legs and whistling by his head.

With no choice, Hearst dived for cover behind the nearest boulder, throwing his hands up and rolling over a shoulder as he slammed to a halt.

A moment later, Nat and Spenser rolled to a halt beside him, a volley of gunshots hurrying them on their way.

Nat sat back against the boulder, facing Hearst.

'Any ideas?' he asked, his voice low.

'Is that Fernandez's gang?'

'Yeah.'

Hearst closed his eyes a moment and took a deep breath.

'Then we got to put aside our differences to get out of this.'

Nat raised his head, but gunfire blasted into the boulder and forced him to duck.

'That makes sense,' he said, frowning. 'What's your plan?'

'I'll cover you while you both get flanking positions on either side of Fernandez's men.' Hearst glanced around, searching for potential cover. Two squat boulders were on either side of them. On judging that a running man could reach them within twenty seconds, he pointed at them. 'Then you cover me while I go for the horses.'

Nat glanced at the boulders, shaking his head, then turned back to Hearst.

'You mean we shoot our way out?'

'Yeah.'

'Typical lawman,' Nat snorted. 'You only think of guns.'

'You claimed that you were once a lawman.'

'I was, but when I moved on, I learnt to think.' Nat tapped his temple. 'And sometimes, negotiation works better.'

'Negotiate,' Hearst murmured, then swung his gun on the top of the boulder, but before he could rip off a single shot, a volley of lead blasted into the rock before him, ripping shards into his face, and he ducked.

'You still want to shoot your way out?' Nat said, grinning.

Hearst removed his hat and poked a finger through a frayed and smouldering bullet hole.

'All right,' he said, slamming the hat back on his head, 'negotiate away.'

'Hey, Fernandez,' Nat shouted, 'why are you shooting at us?'

'You have information,' Fernandez shouted from the top of the ridge. 'And you're giving it to me, one way or the other.'

'We'll tell you about that gold shipment, but only when you lower your guns.'

Nat counted to ten. He glanced up, then smiled at the lack of gunfire.

'You're making a big mistake,' Hearst said, shaking his head. 'You can't trust an outlaw like Fernandez.'

Nat snorted, then stood, followed by Spenser.

Hearst watched them pace out and face up the slope. On the count of twenty, Fernandez's men hadn't ripped out any gunfire, so, with a reluctant shake of his head, he followed them.

From the top of the ridge, Fernandez paced out from his cover and strode down the slope to stand halfway down, facing them. Talbot and Luther flanked him, standing two paces back. But all three men had holstered their guns, as had the men on the ridge.

'And who are you?' Fernandez asked, pointing at Hearst.

Nat glanced at Hearst. 'Don't worry about him. He's no trouble.'

'I asked *him* that question,' Fernandez snapped.

Hearst held his hands wide. 'Like Nathan . . . Nat says. I'm no trouble.'

'But you were searching for them earlier,' Luther said. 'And you had them at gunpoint when we arrived.'

'It was nothing we couldn't deal with,' Nat said.

'We got ourselves into a long-standing argument. But I don't see why you've attacking us.'

'I've been searching for you for two days,' Fernandez said, 'looking for that *inside* information on the shipment.'

'The gold is heading into Bear Creek within the hour.'

Fernandez nodded. 'And its route?'

'It'll head through Deadman's Gulch. It'll have few if any guards and—'

'That'll do.' Fernandez raised a hand, then swung round. He paced back up the slope to join Luther, but then stopped and swirled round to face them. He pointed a firm finger at Nat. 'And you'd better, be right. If you've double-crossed me, you'll live just long enough to regret it.'

'That's the truth.'

Fernandez stood a moment, then clicked his fingers.

Hearst edged his hand towards his holster, but the only response from Fernandez's men was for a portly man to stand then slither down the slope towards them. Before this man reached Fernandez, Hearst recognized him as Dewey Wade.

Fernandez chuckled then ripped his gun from its holster and aimed it down at the threesome, the action faster than any of them could react to.

'But that ain't what Dewey says. He claims that you sold me out to two lawmen.' Fernandez grinned and aimed his gun at Nat's head. 'What you got to say about that?'

CHAPTER 13

As Spenser and Hearst winced, Nat paced forward.

'Fernandez,' he said, 'don't listen to the lies of a saloon bum like Dewey Wade.'

'Except I did listen.' Fernandez stood aside to let Dewey shuffle down the slope and join him, but Dewey kept his eyes downcast. 'And he told me that this man is a lawman, and that you did a deal with him to turn me in for the bounty.'

'We ain't bounty hunters. We *are* bank raiders.' Nat shrugged. 'And did it look like we were working together when you arrived?'

'It didn't. But either way, you're trouble I don't need. So, drop your gunbelts and put those hands high.'

Hearst lowered his hand another inch towards his holster, but Fernandez narrowed his eyes and with a shrug, Hearst unhooked his gunbelt and threw it on the ground, but only a few feet before him. Nat and Spenser did the same.

But, on Fernandez's instructions, Luther paced forward, grabbed the gunbelts, and hurled them over his shoulder.

Fernandez firmed his gun hand and sighted Nat's

forehead. Nat glared down the barrel.

'You can't kill us,' he said. 'We're the only ones who can help you get that gold.'

'But you've told me where it'll be.'

'And what if I lied?'

Fernandez's right eye twitched. 'I know how to make a man talk.'

'Even if you can make me talk, you have less than an hour.'

Fernandez's gun hand shook with a momentary tremor. Then he lowered it.

'Then I have to trust you,' he grunted. 'Tie them up, Luther.'

Luther scurried back up the ridge and gathered rope from his horse, then slithered down the slope to Nat's side.

Nat backed away a pace, but Luther grabbed his arm and pushed him towards the nearest boulder. Nat wheeled to a halt, then whirled round, his fists rising, but Fernandez barked a short command forcing Nat to lower them.

Luther shoved Nat to the ground then, with calm efficiency, secured him to the boulder, crossing the rope back and forth across his chest, then looping it around his arms and legs to ensure he couldn't wriggle out.

Then he secured Hearst and Spenser to the boulders on either side of Nat.

With so many men standing around them, none of them resisted.

'Trust me, Fernandez,' Nat said, when Luther stood back.

'Once I have the gold I might,' Fernandez smirked. 'Except if I do get it, I might not bother to come back and question you. And if I don't get it, you might sit there until you rot, if you're lucky.'

Fernandez gestured up the slope and his men peeled from their positions at the top of the ridge and headed to their horses. As they led their steeds on a snaking path towards them, Fernandez stalked back and forth, tapping a fist against his thigh.

Dewey stared up the slope, but he still flinched every time Fernandez stalked by him.

When the men joined him, Fernandez mounted his horse, Luther and Talbot following him. But when Dewey moved to mount his steed, Fernandez shook his head.

'Can't I go with you?' Dewey whined, his eyes wide and pleading. 'I showed I'm useful this time.'

Fernandez pointed down at the captive men. 'Guard them and prove it.'

Dewey shuffled a slow pace towards the prisoners while Fernandez drew his horse to the side. But Fernandez stayed back while his men found the safest route down to the trail.

Dewey stood before Spenser and eyed the thick bonds securing him to the boulder, then smirked.

'You got to help us, Dewey,' Spenser said, his voice too low for Fernandez to hear.

'Like I said, even I can better myself, and I reckon I'm doin' that. I'm always the outsider.' Dewey puffed his chest and straightened his tattered clothing. 'But now, I'm on the inside.'

'You won't get the chance,' Spenser snapped.

'Fernandez will kill you when he returns, just like he'll kill us.'

'He won't kill me.'

'He will, because of what I'll tell him.'

'Like what?'

Spenser snorted. 'Just help us.'

Dewey folded his arms. 'I ain't doin' nothin'.'

Spenser stared hard at Dewey, but when Dewey just narrowed his eyes, he lifted his head to face Fernandez.

'Hey, Fernandez,' he shouted, 'you know what Dewey really does?'

As the last of his men set off down the slope, Fernandez moved to follow them, but then turned in the saddle to face Spenser.

'Not interested,' he snapped. 'And, Dewey, keep your prisoners quiet.'

'Dewey is a dirty double-crosser,' Spenser shouted, his voice echoing back from the ridge. 'He sold information on you to Sheriff Ballard.'

Dewey slumped to his knees. In an instant, his hands shot up to assume a praying position.

'I didn't, I didn't,' he babbled. 'Don't believe him, Fernandez, please. I didn't. I didn't.'

Fernandez pulled his horse back and paced it in a steady arc around Dewey.

Dewey hung his head until his forehead was six inches from the ground, his pleas drifting to silence, but Fernandez continued past him until he stood over Spenser.

'And don't you think I know that?' he said. 'Dewey has sold useless information to Ballard for the last year – enough to keep the lawman quiet, but not enough to let him get me.'

Spenser glanced at Dewey, who had closed his eyes and pressed his forehead to the dirt while mumbling to himself.

'You knew?' Spenser murmured.

As Fernandez nodded, Dewey raised his head, grit mottling his forehead.

'You mean you ain't angry, boss?' he murmured.

'Nope. Even worthless saloon bums have their uses.' Fernandez raised his reins. 'And that's why I like you. And why I trust you to look after my prisoners.'

Dewey gulped, then peered up at Fernandez. 'And what do I do with them?'

'Whatever you want.' Fernandez chuckled. 'Consider it a test of whether you're an outsider or an insider.'

Fernandez glanced at each of his captives then snorted and rode past Dewey and down the slope, his men in a line before him as they headed for the trail, leaving Dewey to grin and rub his hands.

'Now,' Dewey said, licking his lips as he stood, 'what should I do with some real double-crossers?'

'You fine in there?' Sheriff Ballard said, peering at Cassidy through the cell bars.

'Yep,' Cassidy said.

'You not eager to move on?'

Cassidy glanced at the open cell door, then shrugged and interlocked his hands behind his head as he leaned back on his bunk.

'I'll let justice run its course, like I always do.'

'I don't believe it,' Ballard snorted. 'You're proud of what you did.'

'I'm not. I just made a mistake.'

Ballard ran a finger along the edge of the cell door. He pulled the door open a foot then pushed it back so that it closed.

'But as a result, you're sitting in a cell. And it ain't even locked. You must feel pretty stupid.'

Cassidy shuffled back on to his bunk and drew a leg up to place the knee before his shoulder.

'I ain't the one demeaning himself. I did what I thought was best, but I was wrong and I'll face the consequences in a court of law. But whatever the court decides, I'll still be a better lawman than you'll ever be.'

Ballard threw back his head and snorted a huge guffaw.

'And how did you figure that out?'

'Because you're doing something I'd never do. You're gloating at one of your prisoners. And *that* discredits everything the badge stands for.' Cassidy rocked his leg to the floor and leaned on it. 'If anyone should apologize, it's you.'

'I'm not gloating.' Ballard swung the cell open and stood in the cell doorway. 'I want you to learn humility. And then, when you next ride into another lawman's territory, you won't tell him how to run his town. And you won't ruin his investigations. And you won't shoot up innocent folk when you got no right even being there in the first place.'

With hooded eyes, Cassidy glared at Ballard.

'Grovelling to you won't help none.'

'I guess it won't. You're already too useless. But it doesn't hurt to try.' Ballard glanced at the empty cell beside Cassidy's. 'A pity you ain't got as much sense as your deputy. He understood.'

'Hearst didn't. He left to continue with our investigation.'

Ballard narrowed his eyes and lowered his voice.

'What investigation?'

'Before we tried to find that gold shipment, he was determined to track down Rodrigo Fernandez to reclaim your approval. I talked him out of it. But with me in here, I guess that's what he's doing.'

'He wouldn't ruin another investigation, surely?'

'He won't aim to. But if he's as incompetent as you reckon he is. . . .'

Ballard lowered his head a moment, but then stood tall.

'Hearst won't get close enough to Fernandez to ruin anything.'

'Perhaps not. But he was close enough to learn that the gold shipment was on the train to Denver. And as I now reckon that it came off before we boarded the train, it'll be heading to Bear Creek on the open trail and it'll get here soon, perhaps within the hour. And Fernandez will raid it.'

'If he does, he'll fail.'

'I know, because I also reckon you have another plan to capture him.'

Ballard waved his hand in a dismissive gesture at Cassidy.

'I ain't listening to your wild theories.'

'But I'm right, ain't I?'

For long moments Ballard didn't reply, and when he spoke his voice was low and guarded.

'The gold is coming, today.'

Cassidy rolled from his bunk and stood before Ballard.

'And nothing can go wrong with your plan to get Fernandez, except for a random element, like Isaac Gillespie giving information to two bounty hunters who want Fernandez for themselves, and to a deputy sheriff who has his own plans.'

'Isaac wouldn't talk to Hearst.'

'Isaac will tell anyone anything, for the right price, and as Hearst didn't return here, I guess he got the information he needed and is now closing on Fernandez.'

Ballard gulped and half-turned from Cassidy.

'If you're right, what will he do?'

Cassidy let a smile twitch the corners of his mouth, then yawned and sat back on his bunk.

'What do you care?'

'Just tell me,' Ballard intoned. He swirled back to face Cassidy, his face reddening.

'I'm a prisoner. I got rights.' Cassidy crossed his legs on the bunk and lay flat. 'And I don't have to tell you anything.'

Ballard kicked the cell door open to crash it back against the bars.

'Tell me!' he roared.

'I'm right comfortable. I don't want to talk.' Cassidy yawned and closed his eyes. 'Come back at sundown and I might feel like talking then.'

Ballard stalked into the cell and grabbed Cassidy's collar. He pulled him from the bunk, Cassidy going limp in his grip, then stood him straight.

'You ain't littering up my cell no more.'

Cassidy opened his eyes, then raised his eyebrows.

'That mean you're letting me go?'

'Yeah.' Ballard shoved Cassidy a pace towards the open cell door. 'Now, tell me what your goddamn useless varmint of a deputy will do before I kick you from here to Morbid.'

'Monotony.' Cassidy smoothed his rumpled jacket and smiled. 'But seeing as you asked so nicely. . . .'

'Dewey,' Spenser said, his voice level, 'don't do anything rash.'

'Don't tell me what to do,' Dewey snapped, pointing a firm finger at Spenser.

'Don't let Spenser confuse you,' Nat said. 'We had a deal. You can't go back on it.'

'We only agreed to help each other.' Dewey ran his gaze along the bonds securing Nat to the boulder. 'But Spenser has just ended all that and you ain't in no position to do any helpin' now.'

'You can't try to get into Fernandez's gang one moment, then join us to capture him the next, then switch back.'

'I can.'

'Dewey,' Nat said, 'that's a mighty dangerous plan for someone like you.'

'What you mean – for someone like me?'

'It means you're a no—'

'What Nat means,' Hearst said, interrupting, 'is

that you're too decent a man to be in Fernandez's gang. You're sure to get killed.'

Both Nat and Spenser snorted a harsh chuckle, but Dewey firmed his jaw.

'I'll survive.'

'Or,' Spenser said, 'you could join us. Then, you'll live.'

'Fine talk when you're tied to a boulder.'

Spenser hung his head, but Nat nodded.

'It is,' he said. 'Because Fernandez is within an hour of capture, and without him to protect you, you'll need friends, and we're the nearest you'll get.'

'How is Fernandez gettin' captured?'

'Because we've worked out Sheriff Ballard's plans – the ones he hasn't told you. And we know Isaac Gillespie's plans, the ones—'

'And what are they?'

Nat looked to the sky. 'We're not telling you.'

'You will.' Dewey slapped his chest. 'Then Fernandez will know how invaluable I am.'

'Fernandez told you to deal with us in any way you saw fit. So, until we know you're on our side, we'll say nothing.'

Dewey stared at them, but then scoffed and slumped to the ground to sit facing his prisoners, cross-legged.

'You got no information. So, I'll just guard you until Fernandez returns.'

'But we have maps of the route the gold's taking to Bear Creek, and of where Ballard's ambush will take place.'

Dewey sneered and looked away, his chin held

high. Hearst glanced at Nat and raised his eyebrows, but Nat shook his head and mouthed a cautionary plea for him to say nothing.

Dewey rocked his head from side to side. He mumbled to himself, then leapt to his feet and shuffled five paces up the slope.

But then, with a slap of a fist against his thigh, he stalked down the slope to stand over Nat. He fingered Nat's bonds, then tugged on them, confirming that they pressed Nat tight against the boulder. He peered at Nat's jacket, then hunkered down and ripped it open.

Nat firmed his chest and flinched as far from Dewey's hands as his bonds would allow, but Dewey still rummaged through his pockets. He found nothing, but then his questing hand slipped deep inside Nat's jacket, and his eyes widened.

'Now, what's this?' he chortled.

Dewey leaned down to thrust his hand behind Nat's back, but Nat swung up a long leg and crashed it into the back of Dewey's right knee.

In an involuntary action, Dewey stumbled forward, slamming into Nat's chest and, as he tried to regain his stance by pushing himself from the boulder, Nat entangled his right leg around Dewey's ankles and kicked out. Nat could move only a few inches, but his lunge tumbled Dewey to the side.

As Dewey slammed his hands to the ground to right himself, Nat lunged to the full extent of his reach, just a foot, but it was enough for him to reach Dewey's holster. With a twirl of the wrist, he drew Dewey's gun, then thrust it deep into his guts.

'Dewey,' he whispered, 'make one wrong move and you're dead.'

Dewey gulped and raised his hands. 'What do you want me to do?'

'Cut me free.'

'I . . . I got to get the knife from my horse to do that.'

'Don't try to be clever. It don't suit you. You got a knife in your boot. Use that.'

'How did you know I had a hidden knife there?' Dewey whined.

'Because you just told me.' Nat grinned. 'Now, release me.'

Dewey gulped and, with slow movements, slipped the knife from his boot then sawed through Nat's bonds.

When Dewey had severed the main three bonds, Nat beckoned Dewey to back away then struggled out from the cut rope. He took the knife from Dewey and released Spenser then, after a moment's thought, released Hearst, too.

'Obliged to you,' Hearst said, stretching his back. 'But I—'

Hearst heard frantic footfalls and swirled round to see that Dewey was scurrying up the slope. Spenser followed his gaze and laughed.

'Hey, Dewey,' he shouted. 'Get back here. You're *our* prisoner now.'

But Dewey hunched his shoulders high and, on hands and feet, scampered up the slope. Hearst moved to chase after him, but Nat shook his head.

'Don't,' he said. 'We got no further use for him.'

'Still don't stop us teaching him a lesson,' Spenser muttered. He dashed ten paces up the slope and located his gun, then fired over Dewey's head.

Dewey thrust his head down and hurtled up the last few paces to the top of the ridge, then hurled himself, head first, over the top.

Nat and Spenser glanced at each other, smiling, then turned to Hearst, but the lawman firmed his jaw.

'We may be free,' he said, 'but I still got to take you in, and I don't advise you to take on a lawman.'

'We won't do that,' Nat said. 'But we still got Fernandez to capture before I hand myself in, like I promised.'

'If you're right and Ballard is after Fernandez, I'll leave him to it, but you aren't convincing me that you're going after Fernandez. But you are coming with me to Bear Creek to free Cassidy.'

'I can prove I didn't lie.'

Hearst sneered and pointed down the slope, but when Nat shook his head and folded his arms, he raised his hands.

'All right, for Cassidy's sake, I'll listen. But you got one minute to convince me. And it'd better be good.'

'I can't do it in a minute. But in thirty minutes, you'll see proof that the gold shipment *was* on the train.'

'It wasn't,' Hearst snapped. 'It left long before Cassidy and me boarded that train.'

'It didn't. The shipment was in the transportation carriage and didn't come off until it reached Denver.'

'We were in the transportation carriage,' Hearst shouted. 'And there was no gold.'

'And what *was* in the carriage?'

'Four men playing poker.' Hearst shrugged. 'And a few boxes and crates.'

'And was there a crate big enough to hold the gold shipment?'

'No.' Hearst rubbed his chin. 'Although there was one large crate, but that contained rancid furs.'

Nat snorted a laugh. 'And like Isaac Gillespie said to us, if a dozen guards can't reach Bear Creek without Fernandez raiding them and stealing their shipment, who else can?'

'I don't know. Who can?'

'An old-timer driving a cart loaded down with a single packing crate filled with rancid furs.'

Hearst winced. 'You saying the gold was in that crate, in disguise?'

'I sure am. There may have been a whole heap of furs in it, but the gold underneath them will wash clean. And it'll head down this trail within the hour.'

Hearst winced. 'That's the most ridiculous way of delivering gold I've ever heard.'

'Maybe, but are you still with us?' Nat smiled. 'Or are you letting Fernandez steal it?'

CHAPTER 14

'We're here,' Sheriff Ballard muttered, pulling his horse to a halt. 'So, where's Hearst?'

'He's close,' Cassidy said, drawing his horse alongside Ballard's.

Cassidy glanced up and down the trail, but not a single person interrupted his view. Neither had he seen anyone since he'd left Bear Creek. And although he didn't like to admit it, his hunch that Hearst would have headed towards the last place he'd seen Nat and Spenser was increasingly looking to be false.

Ballard snorted. 'How can you know that?'

'I know my deputy. He's close.'

'But why are you searching this trail, and not the trail to Denver?'

'For once, quit asking questions.'

'You don't give the orders here. Now, just tell me what you're basing your guess on.'

Cassidy ran his gaze along the low hills, searching for the signal Hearst would give him if he were holed up there, waiting for Nat and Spenser, but on seeing nothing, he turned to Ballard.

'The gold shipment came off the train before Hearst and me boarded it. So, it's heading west, and that means—'

'And that means you got no idea what's happening.'

'That ain't true. I know how my deputy will investigate.'

Ballard hurled his hands high. 'You know nothing. You're second-guessing someone who's only good enough to be the deputy to an idiot sheriff.'

Cassidy gritted his teeth. 'I'm following my hunches as to where Hearst went.'

'You ain't got no hunches. And I'm not wasting my time on you no more. You and Hearst are in no position to foul up anything and I'll have Fernandez within the hour.' Ballard aimed a firm finger at Cassidy. 'And then I'll come for you. Don't let me find you or . . .'

'Or what? You got nothing real to charge me with.'

'I'll find something.' Ballard tugged on the reins, pulling his horse round on the trail. 'Now, go!'

Ballard spurred his horse for speed and hurtled back towards the Denver trail, his horse throwing up great plumes of dust behind him.

Cassidy watched Ballard leave, confirming that he didn't look back even once.

He glanced over his shoulder at the trail stretching ahead towards Monotony, then again at the hills, looking, for the last time, for a signal.

On seeing nothing, he shrugged and nudged his horse into following Ballard at a steady trot.

*

117

'And that's the gold shipment, is it?' Hearst muttered.

'Yep,' Nat said, peering down the slope.

A cart was approaching, a haggard, round-shoul-dered old-timer driving. On the back of the cart, wide ropes secured a battered crate – the same crate that Hearst had seen in the transportation carriage.

Hearst narrowed his eyes, confirming that the driver was Art Weston, the man who Cassidy had confronted on the train.

And even from 200 yards away, the light breeze ensured that the rancid smell emerging from the crate polluted Hearst's nostrils.

'Then,' Hearst said, 'I suppose we got to head down there and help that old-timer.'

Nat nodded and the three men paced out from their cover and shuffled down the slope, Spenser bringing up the rear and holding their horses. Hearst took the lead and, with a hand raised, stood on the side of the trail.

With a long holler and a firm pulling back on the reins, Weston stopped fifty yards from them. He leaned forward and peered at Hearst while holding the reins in one hand and slapping his other hand on the rifle that lay on the seat beside him.

'That be close enough,' he shouted. 'What d'you want?'

'I don't aim to cause you no trouble,' Hearst shouted.

'You might not, but a man who packs a gun and stands on the trail is lookin' to be shot. So, keep those hands high.'

Hearst raised his hands, then gestured for Nat and Spenser to also raise their hands.

Hearst sniffed. 'That crate sure smells ripe.'

'What smell?' Weston shrugged. 'But I got me a delivery to make. So, if you ain't trouble, move aside and I won't give you none.'

Hearst provided a welcoming smile. 'Good. Isaac Gillespie wouldn't like that.'

Weston flinched. 'What you gettin' at?'

'You're delivering to Isaac and he sent us on ahead to help you deliver his *furs*.'

'I've taken these furs nigh on five hundred miles, no problem, no problem at all – people don't want to come close to them. So, I don't need no help for the last twenty miles.'

'Isaac thinks that you might, Art Weston.'

'How d'you know my name?'

'Like I said – Isaac Gillespie sent us to help you.'

'And why would he do that for a heap of old furs?'

'Because Rodrigo Fernandez is around and he's waylaying people on the trail.'

Weston narrowed his eyes. 'My eyes ain't what they used to be, but I recognize you now. You were with that trigger-happy sheriff on the train.'

'I wasn't trouble then and I ain't trouble now. I just want this shipment to reach Bear Creek safely.'

'You're goin' to a mighty lot of trouble for a heap of old furs,' Weston said. 'No matter what that sheriff said, there ain't no gold in that crate.'

Hearst glanced at the crate. 'Maybe there is, or maybe there ain't. But either way, it's less than an hour to Bear Creek, and we ought to be able to find a way to work together for that long.'

Weston leaned from the side of the cart to spit on the ground, then appraised the three men. He provided a sharp nod.

'I guess I got room for three young 'uns.'

'Obliged.'

Weston shook the reins and hurried his horses on to draw alongside Hearst then gestured for them to climb on the back of the cart.

Hearst sniffed then sat beside Weston. Nat vaulted on to the back, but he sat as far from the crate as he could. Spenser mounted his horse, and when Weston shook the reins, he rode alongside, trailing their horses behind them as they headed down the trail towards Bear Creek.

'When you expectin' Fernandez to raid?' Weston asked.

'He's holed up in Deadman's Gulch,' Hearst said.

'Then I'll take the longer route and avoid him – there's a turnin' four miles on.'

Hearst smiled. 'That pretty much sums up our plans for avoiding trouble.'

CHAPTER 15

For three miles, Weston drove the cart at a steady pace. He also maintained a steady prattle about his journey, which, aside from Cassidy knocking the conductor out of the moving train, had been dull.

Hearst encouraged the conversation, as talking to Weston gave him plenty of opportunities to look around and check where Spenser and Nat were. But even though he couldn't shake the nagging fear that these men had an ulterior motive in accompanying the gold shipment, every mile that passed got them closer to Bear Creek and helped to calm his suspicions.

And, when the turning that avoided Deadman's Gulch appeared ahead, Hearst was even enjoying Weston's jabbering.

But then hard metal thrust into the centre of Hearst's back.

Hearst flinched, the action shaking him from the benign torpor into which he'd sunk, but even as he slipped his hand towards his gun, Nat ripped it from Hearst's holster and hurled it over his shoulder.

Hearst flexed, ready to swirl round and grab Nat,

but at the side of the cart, Spenser swung in and trained his gun on him.

At his side, Weston snorted, but held the reins high as he watched Nat thrust the metal in further.

'Do nothing,' Nat muttered. 'I was once a deputy and I got no desire to kill one.'

'And I got no idea why Cassidy hired a no-good varmint like you,' Hearst snapped, raising his hands. 'Or why he still trusts you.'

'I'm not looking for no understanding from you. I just want Weston to stop this cart. Then you're leaving us.'

At the side of the cart, Spenser firmed his gun hand, but Weston stared straight ahead and rode on for another fifty yards.

But, in response to another barked command from Nat, Weston turned and considered Nat's firm-jawed gaze. He spat over the side of the cart, then pulled back on the reins, halting the cart.

'And what about me?' he muttered.

'You'll go with Deputy Hearst,' Nat said, shrugging.

'I don't know about no gold shipment, but I'm to deliver that crate, and this cart is mine. And I ain't lettin' any of them go.'

'We don't aim to—'

'Nat,' Spenser muttered, 'just take the reins.'

'We're not robbing this old-timer, too.' Nat sighed, then lowered his voice. 'What will keep you quiet, old-timer?'

'I'll drive the cart for you, young 'un. Then, when you've unloaded your gold, if it's there, I'll keep the cart and the furs.'

Spenser snorted. 'We can't agree to—'

'We will,' Nat said. 'You can come with us, old . . . Weston.'

Weston glanced at Hearst, shrugged, then folded up the brim of his hat.

'I ain't no outlaw,' he said. 'I don't want no posse after me.'

Hearst provided a sharp nod then, to Nat's directions, jumped down from the cart.

'I always knew,' Hearst said, as Nat rolled into the seat beside Weston, 'that you were lying when you promised Cassidy you'd get Fernandez.'

'That ain't so,' Nat said. 'I'll do everything I promised. Spenser will leave your horse a mile along the trail, and as it's only fifteen miles to Bear Creek, you got plenty of time to get back there.'

'I won't head back to Bear Creek. I'll come for you, and I won't rest until I find you.'

'You won't follow me.' Nat nudged Weston into circling the horses around Hearst. 'Rodrigo Fernandez is in Deadman's Gulch waiting to ambush this gold, and, as it ain't coming, he'll be there for awhile. But if you fetch Sheriff Ballard and raise a posse, you'll capture him, no trouble. You can't chase both of us. It's either Fernandez or us. And I reckon you'll choose Fernandez.'

'I guess I will,' Hearst shouted, swirling round on the spot so that he continued to face Nat. 'But that's even worse news for you, Nathaniel. It means Marshal Devine will be on your trail.'

Nat ordered Weston to pull back on the reins, halt-

ing the horses with the cart directed away from
Deadman's Gulch.

'That don't worry me. Devine will never get me.'

Hearst glanced at Spenser, who was now on the
other side of the cart, then turned away from Nat to
stare back down the trail. But, as Nat turned to face
the front, he swirled round on his heel and broke
into a run.

In four long paces, Hearst reached the cart and, as
Weston shook the reins and the horses broke into a
trot, he leapt at Nat, grabbed his arm, and tried to
pull him from the cart.

On the edge of his seat, Nat teetered, but then dug
his heels in and pulled back.

Hearst bounded along beside the cart, then
relented from pulling and instead, leapt on to the
seat. He sprawled over Nat and tumbled him into the
back of the cart, but Nat grabbed a trailing arm and
dragged Hearst with him.

While swinging his horse round the back of the
cart, Spenser ordered Weston to stop. But as the cart
slowed, Hearst ripped his arm from Nat's grip, then
dragged Nat to his feet and slugged his jaw with a
sharp uppercut. Nat's head snapped back, and he
tottered back a pace.

Hearst lunged for Nat's gun, but then a heavy
weight slammed into his back and knocked him
against the crate. He'd just realized that Spenser had
jumped him when a second blow to the cheek sent
him spinning along the side of the crate.

Hearst shrugged off the blow and swirled round, but
faced the two men, who advanced on him, fists raised.

Spenser threw the first punch. Hearst ducked it, but when he bobbed up, Nat hurled a blow at his face. He couldn't avoid this one and it thundered into his cheek, hurling him into one of the ropes that secured the crate. With no control of his movements, he folded over the rope, slid down it, then tumbled over the side of the cart, landing in a sprawled heap on the ground.

In the cart, Nat shouted to Weston to hurry and, as Hearst sat up, the cart lurched into motion, then hurtled away from him at a gallop.

Hearst staggered to his feet, swayed, then dashed after the cart, shouting taunts at Nat.

But after 200 yards or so, the cart was well ahead of him and he stomped to a halt, then slapped his hat to the ground.

'I'll make you regret that, Nathaniel,' he muttered, kicking dirt. 'I surely will.'

For around a mile, Weston rode at a steady pace, but then on Nat's instructions, he pulled back on the reins beside an overgrown cottonwood tree. There, Spenser tethered Hearst's horse, then secured their horses to the back of the cart while Nat removed the crate lid and peered inside, wincing at the rank smell emerging from within as he rummaged.

He smiled, then replaced the lid and, when Spenser joined him in sitting beside the crate, Weston shook the reins.

At a steadier pace, they headed north.

'Is it in there?' Spenser asked.

'The gold is under the furs, like Isaac said.'

At the front of the cart, Weston snorted.

'Good.' Spenser frowned. 'But is Devine as good as Hearst reckons?'

'Yeah,' Nat said. 'You'll need to put as much distance between you and him as possible.'

'*We* need to, you mean.'

'Nope, just you. I'm going back. That's what I promised Cassidy, and that's what I'll do.'

'And what about your promises to me?'

'I said I'd deliver on all my promises, and I will. I've ensured Rodrigo Fernandez gets justice, like I promised Cassidy. I've helped you get the gold, like I promised you. And when I'm sure you've escaped, I'll turn myself in.'

'Like you promised both of us,' Spenser murmured. 'But you helped me raid this gold shipment. For that, you'll get life.'

'I don't think so. You'll have the gold, not me.'

'You still helped.'

'Yeah, but I reckon Isaac Gillespie won't want too many people knowing he entrusted that much gold to an old-timer and a smelly crate, then told two bounty hunters about his plan. He'll downplay the incident, and with me giving myself in, I reckon I'll just get the five years I thought I'd get.'

'I guess so.' Spenser patted Nat's back, then firmed his jaw and stared back down the trail. 'And don't worry yourself in jail. When you find me, I won't have spent your share.'

'I know. You've given your word.'

Spenser rolled to his haunches and peered around. 'How far are we going until you leave?'

Nat glanced over his shoulder, seeing nothing but the deserted trail behind, although a dust cloud on the horizon drew his gaze.

'Just until I'm sure that we're safe.'

'And when will that be?'

Nat narrowed his eyes, watching the cloud spread, although as yet, he saw no hint that it was anything but dust. He leaned forward and pointed at the cloud, but then a distant rifle shot sounded, forcing Nat to swirl round and order Weston to speed.

Spenser joined Nat in narrowing his eyes and peering at the cloud, which even as they stared resolved into a row of riders. Their forms were distant, but from the huge amount of dust they were throwing up, they had to be galloping down the trail and heading straight for them.

'To answer your question,' Nat murmured, 'it ain't any time soon.'

CHAPTER 16

Cassidy pulled his horse to a slow trot.

Fifty yards ahead, Hearst was wandering down the trail, his back bowed and his gait slow.

Cassidy hollered on ahead, forcing Hearst to turn and watch him approach.

'Mighty pleased to see you,' Hearst said, looking up at Cassidy with a huge smile emerging. 'You apologize to Ballard?'

'Nope.' Cassidy halted his horse. 'But I ain't so pleased to see you. I thought you were searching for Nathaniel and Spenser.'

'Found 'em, got double-crossed by 'em. That's why I'm walking.'

Cassidy winced. 'You sure?'

'I know what being double-crossed feels like. And the sooner you start believing that Nathaniel . . .' – Hearst snorted – 'Nat ain't to be trusted, we'll both stop getting tricked so often.'

'You must have misunderstood what—'

'No misunderstanding, Cassidy. Nat thrust a gun in my back and abandoned me on the trail.'

'Nathaniel must have had his reasons.'

'Yeah. He's a no-good outlaw.'

Cassidy stared down the trail a moment, then sighed and held out a hand to Hearst.

'Anyhow, we'll have to ride double.'

'Yeah, but it might not be for long. Nat said he left my horse another half-mile down the trail, if you can believe that.'

'You can. And that just proves who he is. No outlaw would do that.'

'Nat did. But it won't help him none.' Hearst grabbed Cassidy's hand and with his help, swung up on to the back of Cassidy's horse. 'Five minutes ago, Sheriff Ballard and a whole heap of deputies hurtled by. And from the way Ballard was smirking, it didn't look like he was in the mood for Nat's stories.'

Cassidy winced and hurried his horse on ahead.

'They're closing,' Spenser shouted.

'Go faster,' Nat grunted, swirling round to confront Weston. 'I let you drive this cart because you had more experience. Show it!'

'No matter how much experience I got,' Weston shouted, 'we'll never outrun those riders in the open plains.'

'Then head for cover and we'll make a stand.'

Weston glanced around, his gaze washing over the barren wilderness.

'What cover?'

Nat winced. 'Then keep going until we *do* find some.'

Another glance over his shoulder convinced Nat that the horses *were* closing and that Sheriff Ballard led the group, presumably of deputies.

Seemingly with every turn of the wheels, Ballard drew closer, but as the deputies held their fire, Spenser shuffled closer to Nat.

'You got a decision to make,' he said. 'Are we firing?'

'We return fire to defend ourselves,' Nat said. 'But we don't start no gunfight.'

'Nat, I hope you know what you're doing.'

Nat narrowed his eyes, confirming that Ballard *was* gaining fast. He looked over his shoulder at Weston's horses to see that they were galloping, but they weren't straining.

He winced and shuffled to the front of the cart, then vaulted into the seat alongside Weston.

'Speed up!' he roared.

'I'm goin' as fast as I can,' Weston shouted, shaking the reins with a huge crack of his bony arms.

'You ain't. You're making a big show of going fast, but your horses ain't straining.'

Weston shrugged. 'I know my horses, and they won't go no faster than this.'

Nat slapped a hand on Weston's arm.

'Whose side are you on?'

Weston stared straight ahead a moment, but then turned to Nat.

'I guess that depends.'

'On what?'

Weston licked his lips, then glared at Nat's hand.

'On whether you're comin' peacefully.'

'I ain't giving in, Weston.'

Weston smiled. 'That's Deputy Weston to you.'

Nat winced, but in a lithe action, Weston dropped the reins and hurled a wild blow at Nat's head. Nat ducked the blow, but with the reins dangling free, the horses slowed with every pace.

Nat lunged for the reins, but Weston grabbed him in a neck-hold and they fell back against the seat, the action tumbling them into the back of the cart.

Spenser moved to help Nat, but Nat shook his head and, seeing his concern, Spenser leapt into the seat and grabbed the reins.

On their knees, Nat and Weston rocked back and forth. Then Weston tightened his grip of Nat's neck and, with surprising strength, tugged him down, but Nat grabbed Weston's arm, halting his progress then pried it from his neck. Grunting from the effort, Nat pushed him away.

Weston rocked back on his haunches, then rolled forward and hurled a round-armed blow at Nat's head.

Nat ducked the blow and when he came up, he slugged Weston's jaw with a sharp uppercut that snapped his head back, and a longer blow to the cheek that knocked him on his back.

Then he jumped to his feet and swirled round.

Even though Spenser had now grabbed the reins and was speeding the horses, Ballard and his deputies were within fifty yards of flanking them.

A heavy blow smashed into Nat's back, slamming his head into the crate. Nat grunted and pushed himself back, but Weston grabbed a firm grip of the back of his head and mashed his face into the wood.

Nat waved his arms, floundering as he searched

for some part of Weston's body to grab, but his grasp closed on air. Then he stamped back, and his flailing boot crunched into Weston's foot.

Weston screeched and his grip loosened, letting Nat swirl round, but even as he pushed Weston away, Ballard's deputies hurried on to the flank the cart.

One deputy swung in and leapt on to the back of the cart, landing on his feet before his sideways momentum rolled him on to his side.

As the deputy struggled to regain his stance, Nat jumped over one of the ropes that secured the crate to reach the man's side. Using both hands, he grabbed a firm grip of the deputy's arm and shoulder, then flung him from the back of the cart.

But as the man tumbled away, another deputy leapt on to the cart behind Nat and as Nat swirled round to face him, this man righted himself and grabbed Nat in a neck-hold from behind. With a firm lunge, he thrust Nat's arms high.

Nat kicked back, aiming to stamp on the deputy's foot, but the deputy had his feet set firm and avoided the blow.

With a solid thrust of his boot in the back of Nat's knee, the deputy pushed Nat to his knees, then tried to force him on to his belly.

Nat flexed his back and sat tall, but it was only to face Weston, who rolled to his feet and advanced on Nat with a fist raised.

Weston hurled back a fist, ready to punch Nat in the guts, but Nat thrust his head down, throwing the deputy over his shoulder and bundling him into Weston.

Both deputies landed heavily, their limbs entangled as they rolled over each other, but they extricated themselves then advanced on Nat with their hands raised ready for a joint action to capture him.

Nat backed away. The two deputies closed on him, blocking his route in either direction, but Nat slammed a hand on the crate and vaulted over the side. He landed on his feet on the other side, but it was only to face another deputy, who had leapt on to the cart, and this man slugged his jaw.

Nat shrugged off the blow, but Weston dashed around the side of the crate to confront him. Nat backed away but walked into the other deputy who emerged from the other end of the crate. And this man locked both hands together and crashed them down on the back of Nat's shoulders, tumbling him down.

As Nat floundered on the bottom of the cart, all three deputies leapt on him and with rough hands, pinned him down.

Through the tangle of arms and legs, Nat saw that another deputy had joined Spenser on the seat and had wrested the reins from his grasp to slow the cart.

For his part, Spenser had his hands held high, a row of gun-wielding deputies who were now flanking the cart having him in their sights.

Then the cart lurched to a halt and, to a barked order from Ballard, the bodies on Nat lifted.

Nat shrugged himself clear, ready to leap to his feet and make a last stand.

But by the back of the cart, Sheriff Ballard had

aimed his Peacemaker at his head, his gaze and arm firm.

Nat glanced over his shoulder to see two deputies were leading Spenser around the side of the cart. Nat slumped, but the deputies on the cart dragged him to his feet. Rough hands gripped his arms and pulled him to the ground to stand alongside Spenser.

'So,' Ballard said, grinning, 'you're the outlaw Nathaniel McBain?'

'Nat McBain.'

'Whatever your name, you're ending up in the same place.'

'But don't waste your time on us,' Nat said, raising his head. 'We got information on Rodrigo Fernandez. But it's only good for another hour, maybe less. Then you'll never get him.'

'I don't need your information to track down the likes of him.'

Ballard swaggered away, leaving his deputies to search Nat and Spenser, then handcuff them.

Spenser glanced at Nat, who shrugged.

'Guess this will be rough,' Nat murmured.

Spenser nodded, but Weston turned him to face down the trail. He winced.

'Yeah, but the next two minutes could be even worse for you.' Spenser nodded ahead.

At a gallop, two riders were approaching.

Nat narrowed his eyes, then looked skyward.

'Cassidy,' he murmured.

CHAPTER 17

Twenty yards from the cart, Cassidy pulled his horse to a halt. He avoided looking directly at the bound Nat and Spenser, although from the corner of his eye, he could see that Nat had the grace to hang his head.

'Am I welcome, Ballard?' he shouted.

'Yeah,' Ballard said. He turned from his appraisal of his prisoners and waved his arms wide. 'You can see what a successful lawman looks like before you head back to Morbid.'

'Monotony.'

Ballard pointed down the trail towards Bear Creek.

'Either way, if you want more tips, come with me. I got Rodrigo Fernandez and the rest of the worthless outlaws in my county to round up.'

Cassidy took a deep breath. 'Ballard, we've had our disagreements, but when a fellow lawman faces an outlaw like Fernandez, I'm prepared to put aside those differences so that Hearst and me can help you.'

'Now, that's mighty generous of you.'

Cassidy searched Ballard's gaze for sarcasm, but detected only joy, and perhaps the hint of another putdown.

'My offer is genuine. Two extra guns might help you get Fernandez.'

'They won't. But you can watch how a real lawman gets the job done. It might help you in Morbid.'

'Mon . . .' Cassidy gritted his teeth. 'Obliged.'

Cassidy and Hearst gave Ballard room to complete his arrangements for moving out. Then, with Nat and Spenser held on the back of the cart with five deputies guarding them, they headed back towards Bear Creek.

The deputies rode with calm precision, a tension in their stiff backs and quiet demeanour. And this anticipation helped Cassidy to avoid looking at Nat, especially when there was nothing he could say to a friend who had obviously double-crossed him.

Hearst had told Cassidy that Rodrigo Fernandez would be lying in wait in Deadman's Gulch. So, as they approached the gulch, Cassidy joined Hearst in increasing his vigilance, peering at every rock that they passed, and listening and looking for any signals that might warn them about an approaching ambush.

But none of Ballard's deputies showed any signs of looking for that ambush.

At the edge of Deadman's Gulch, Ballard halted everyone and called his deputies in for a discussion. He didn't invite Cassidy.

Just as they were disbanding, from ahead, gunfire sounded, the reports crisp and echoing down the gulch.

Ballard looked into the gulch a moment, then ordered Nat and Spenser to jump down from the back of the cart. He let them mount horses, still handcuffed, then directed two deputies to escort his prisoners on the southern, and longer, route around the gulch.

As Ballard clearly had no interest in using him in his attempt to arrest Fernandez, Cassidy offered to accompany them instead of the deputies, but Ballard refused the offer.

Then Ballard ordered Deputy Weston to continue his abortive mission to drive the cart into Bear Creek, but ordered him and an accompanying deputy to use a longer route around the northern part of the gulch.

Then, with the safety of the gold and his prisoners assured, Ballard led his deputies into Deadman's Gulch.

They galloped down the gulch, Ballard leading, and Cassidy and Hearst trailing.

About a half-mile down the gulch, Ballard called everyone to a halt. Around the next bend in the gulch, sustained gunfire was ripping out, so Ballard sent a scout to investigate.

At the back of the troop of deputies, Hearst and Cassidy had a terse discussion. Then Cassidy rode on ahead to join Ballard.

'I know you got no respect for me,' he said, as he watched the scout crawl towards the last rock before the bend. 'But I got some ideas as to—'

Ballard raised a hand. 'That's the first thing you've said that I've agreed with: I *don't* have no respect for you. And I don't need your help either. This situation is under control.'

'There's a fierce gunfight ahead. I assume that Fernandez is ambushing someone, perhaps another group of your deputies, and—'

'And it's *my* deputies who are ambushing Fernandez.

And it's under control.' Ballard waggled a finger at Cassidy. 'Watch and learn.'

Cassidy glared at Ballard a moment, then sighed and backed his horse. As he joined Hearst, the scout returned and relayed his information to Ballard.

From Ballard's grin, Cassidy judged that everything was, in fact, under control.

Ballard ordered his deputies to flank the sides of the gulch and take positions behind every spare bit of cover, ensuring that Cassidy and Hearst hid furthest from the gunfire.

Ahead, the gunfire lessened, fading to sporadic bursts. Then it ripped out again. With every fresh volley, the noise grew louder, suggesting that the shooters were closing.

Ballard stood a moment to wave at his deputies, relaying a silent order that Cassidy assumed told them to hold fire.

Then a straggling line of riders galloped around the bend, firing over their shoulders at assailants that Cassidy couldn't see. Cassidy recognized the lead man as being Luther and two of the men behind him were men who had tried to kill him in the trading post.

These men hurtled through the phalanx of hidden deputies, but when Luther was halfway between the bend and Cassidy's position, Ballard, then his deputies, bobbed up and blasted gunfire into them.

In the first hail of gunfire, the leading five men all went down. The two that the deputies had only wounded rolled to their feet and scampered for cover.

But they were dead before they reached it.

The riders behind this group pulled back and

bunched, prancing their horses round as they yelled at each other, debating whether to risk the gauntlet of steel or return and face the deputies behind them.

Although they were out of easy firing range, Ballard ordered his men to harry them into panicking.

As gunfire peppered the rocks around them, one rider headed up the side of the gulch. But his mount protested at the steep climb and threw him for him to roll and flop to a halt at the gulch bottom. The rest, seeing his failure, galloped back down the gulch and around the bend.

More gunfire blasted, then shouting echoed, then silence.

Ballard stood, cupping his ear, then gestured for his deputies to mount up and head after them.

Cassidy returned his gun to its holster, having failed to fire a single shot, then followed.

When he rounded the bend, he saw a huddle of men standing on the rocks around the gulch bottom with a smaller group below them. And from the guns aimed at these men, and from the hunched way they stood, Cassidy surmised that Fernandez's men had surrendered.

And from the splay of bodies that slowly revealed themselves further down the gulch, these were the lucky ones.

Ballard leapt down from his horse and embarked on a series of backslapping and handshakes.

Then, while his deputies handcuffed the prisoners then herded them on to their horses, he checked on the dead outlaws, discovering that Fernandez was amongst the dead.

Ballard let rip with a joyous whoop that echoed down the gulch, then let the deputy who claimed the kill gather Fernandez's hat for a trophy.

Cassidy and Hearst stood back and, within ten minutes, the well-tethered prisoners were ready to move out. So, at a trot, the group set off down the remaining two miles of Deadman's Gulch, heading to Bear Creek.

At the back, Cassidy glanced around, searching the slopes for any stragglers who may have run when they realized they faced imminent capture, but saw nobody, and Ballard didn't think the effort worthwhile.

Instead, Ballard whistled a merry tune, his deputies hollering and cheering their success. The contented cries echoed down the gulch, heralding their passage.

On the plains, Ballard called a halt and they waited for the deputies that he'd sent around the north and south of the gulch to rejoin them.

As they waited, Ballard rode up and down, nodding to his men. And improbable stories of brav-ery gathered momentum as each man encouraged the others to provide more details about their role in their defeat of Rodrigo Fernandez.

Cassidy and Hearst dismounted and stayed back, avoiding another confrontation, but Ballard rode up to them and raised his eyebrows.

'Your men are a credit to you,' Cassidy said, jutting his jaw. 'And I mean that.'

'Just three usual deputies,' Ballard said, gesturing back at his men, 'and the good folk of Bear Creek make up the rest. So, you learnt enough about being a lawman yet to help you back in Morbid?'

Cassidy glanced at Hearst, who was gritting his teeth.

'I guess I have,' Cassidy grunted.

'Good.' Ballard dismounted and puffed his chest. 'Perhaps you might make a lawman one day. But only if you stop chasing around and learn to plan.'

'You didn't plan all this. You got lucky and trapped Fernandez through his own greed.'

'I *did* plan all this. Isaac Gillespie told me that Nathaniel and Spenser had visited the bank. But I let them carry on with their plans, knowing they'd pass on more information than the bits I'd fed to Dewey Wade, and convince Fernandez to hide out where I wanted him to.'

'You knew Dewey was double-crossing you when he gave you information about Rodrigo Fernandez?'

'Of course.' Ballard chuckled, than patted his stomach and laughed aloud. 'That idiot thought he was leading me on, but when you deal with the likes of Dewey, you learn to extract the truth from all the half-truths and lies. When you understand men like him, you can play everybody to do your bidding.'

'And Dewey will suffer for those lies, one day,' Hearst said. 'He double-crossed Nat, Spenser, and me, too. He told Fernandez that we were trying to capture him.'

'And why didn't Fernandez kill you?' Ballard asked.

'I reckon he was testing Dewey to see if he had the courage to kill us. He tied us up and left Dewey guarding us, but Dewey came too close. Nat knocked his legs from under him and overpowered him.'

'You were tied up and he still couldn't control you!' Ballard threw back his head and roared with laughter. 'That man really is an idiot.'

'If Dewey were as big an idiot as you reckon he is,' Cassidy said, 'he'd never have survived for as long as he has.'

'Fernandez tolerated him. I tolerated him. That mouse survived in the cracks between us.'

'And now,' Hearst said, 'I guess he won't be improving himself like he wanted to.'

Cassidy wandered in a circle, patting his leg, then stopped and stared at Ballard, who was still chuckling.

'Or maybe he was waiting for the right moment to improve himself.'

'What you mean?' Ballard asked.

'I mean you knew what Nathaniel, Spenser and Fernandez wanted.' Cassidy set his hands on his hips. 'But what did Dewey want?'

'Another drink.'

'He did,' Cassidy said. 'But what if that ain't the full story? What if all the time you were playing him, he was playing you?'

'He couldn't,' Ballard said. 'He's an idiot.'

'Dewey was resourceful enough to get a message to Nathaniel, then hold Hearst and me at gunpoint, but he was so stupid he couldn't defeat three bound men. That doesn't sound right.'

'You never know with an idiot like Dewey.' Ballard laughed. 'But I guess an idiot like you would understand him.'

'Either way,' Cassidy said, raising his eyebrows, 'Dewey ain't around.'

'That's not unexpected. I guess he's crawled into some hole.'

'But the gold shipment ain't here either.'

'And,' Hearst said, 'neither are Nat and Spenser.'

'They all took the longer route, so it ain't surprising that—' Ballard gulped and closed his eyes a moment. 'You saying Dewey's ambushed the gold shipment?'

'He knew all the plans. And with Fernandez out of the way . . .'

'And perhaps,' Hearst said, 'he didn't want to kill Nat and Spenser either, and his stupidity was just a show for me.'

'And now he's using that freedom to free Nathaniel and Spenser.'

'I don't believe any of this,' Ballard snapped. 'Dewey ain't resourceful enough to do anything but drink the saloon dry.'

Cassidy swung round to confront Ballard.

'Then answer this – if everything is fine, where's the gold shipment?'

Ballard turned to stare down Deadman's Gulch, then at the plains on either side. He winced, then swirled back to face Cassidy.

'It's on its way. Deputy Weston will be here any minute.'

'Or maybe Deputy Weston has himself a sore head and Dewey is galloping away with more gold than an idiot like him count.'

CHAPTER 18

Ballard directed two deputies to head north around Deadman's Gulch and see what had happened to the men guarding Nat and Spenser, then ordered the other deputies to take the surviving members of Fernandez's men into Bear Creek.

Then he, along with Cassidy and Hearst, headed around the southern route at a gallop.

Within five minutes, they reached the spot where Cassidy judged that the cart would be if it were still heading to Bear Creek.

Ballard remained quiet, but from the way the veins in his neck pulsed as he bunched his jaw, Cassidy reckoned that he thought they should have met it, too.

Still, they rode on for another five minutes. Then Ballard spread them out to flank the low-lying hills on either side of the trail.

But after twenty minutes, they reached the entrance to Deadman's Gulch where they had left Deputy Weston.

There, they scouted around until they found the cart tracks then doubled-back and followed them towards Bear Creek.

But within a half-mile, the tracks left the trail.

They followed the tracks up the slope leading to the gulch and through a grouping of boulders.

A short, silent search found Weston and the other deputy lying unconscious in the shadow of a boulder.

Behind them, the cart tracks led up the slope, but then veered to the side and away from the gulch.

Ballard checked that his deputies were breathing easily, then followed the tracks.

For the next twenty minutes, they followed the tracks on a convoluted path as they skirted round hillocks and crags, taking figure-of-eight patterns, and even doubling back in some sections.

'What in tarnation is that idiot doing?' Ballard grunted, as they rounded a huge crag.

Hearst shrugged. 'Perhaps stealing the gold unhinged what was left of Dewey's mind and he just wandered around.'

'Stop calling Dewey an idiot,' Cassidy said. 'He's the only one who knows everything that happened here.'

Cassidy put his hand to his brow and traced back along the recent path of the tracks, then forward.

He pointed ahead and, with their brows furrowed, Hearst and Ballard followed the direction of his gaze, then urged their horses onward.

One hundred yards on, they saw what Cassidy had pointed at.

The cart tracks stopped.

'The cart can't just disappear,' Ballard said.

'It can't,' Cassidy said. 'But I reckon that by now Dewey had help to brush away the wheel markings.'

'Nat and Spenser?' Hearst asked.

'That's my guess.'

'Clearing away tracks would have taken some effort and a lot of time.' Hearst gazed along the path beyond where the tracks stopped. 'If we carry on, we have to pick up their trail before too long.'

Ballard jumped down from his horse and peered at the end of the wheel tracks and at the flattened dirt where Nat and Spenser, presumably, had scuffed away the wheel markings.

But within ten yards, the scuffing diminished in intensity until the ground returned to its normal gentle undulations.

'The cart could have gone left, right, or straight on,' Ballard said. 'But they couldn't have cleared the tracks away for ever. I'm with Hearst. We just have to scout around and pick them up when they restart.'

'Let me see the tracks,' Cassidy said, dismounting. 'See if I can spot anything.'

'You can't see anything. They covered them well.'

Cassidy hunkered down beside Ballard and peered at the ground, confirming that whoever had removed the markings had been skilful.

He fingered the dirt, then grabbed a handful and let it sprinkle through his fingers.

'Or perhaps too well,' he mused.

'What you mean?'

Cassidy stood and peered around, searching for nearby landmarks. The nearest was the crag behind him.

Cassidy shielded his eyes and saw that halfway up the crag, there was a short ledge and at the back of this, the topmost part of a small cave was visible.

'Nathaniel has taken the gold up there,' he said, pointing.

Ballard joined Cassidy in considering the crag, then turned on the spot searching for likely directions that the cart could have taken.

'You can't know that.'

'I know Nathaniel. He's clever. A cart loaded down with gold can't outrun us even if it takes us hours to pick up the trail. But what if the gold ain't gone anywhere?'

Ballard paced away from Cassidy and stared at the ground that had either had the wheel tracks removed with some skill, or had never had wheel tracks, then shrugged.

With his eyes narrowed, he paced back along the tracks, heading towards the crag.

Fifty feet from the point where the tracks disappeared, he snorted and beckoned Cassidy to join him.

Cassidy scurried down the tracks and stood beside him. He narrowed his eyes and saw that a single wheel track veered off from the normal set of tracks, before it disappeared, too.

'You're right,' Ballard said, hunkering down. He gestured in an arc along the tracks then towards the crag. 'They backed the cart along the wheel tracks they'd just made, then headed to that crag.'

'Then doubled back to wipe away those markings,' Cassidy said, nodding, 'hoping that we'd think they'd continued on the same route.'

Cassidy turned and paced towards the crag, but Ballard jumped to his feet and slapped a hand on his arm, halting him.

'Before we get the gold back, what else . . .' Ballard hung his head a moment, sighing, then met Cassidy's gaze. 'What else do you know about this Nathaniel McBain that'll make our ambush easier for us, Sheriff Yates?'

CHAPTER 19

Cassidy stared at Ballard a moment, but on detecting no sign of sarcasm in his steady gaze, he nodded his thanks.

'I know enough about Nathaniel McBain to take him without bloodshed.' Cassidy took a deep breath. 'But it might be best if I lead, and you back me up.'

Ballard narrowed his eyes. 'You ain't leading.'

'I know Nathaniel.' Cassidy smiled. 'And I always like to have someone I can trust backing me up, Sheriff Ballard.'

Ballard flared his eyes, but then glanced away and nodded.

So, with Hearst and Ballard flanking him, Cassidy headed to the crag.

From the base, he confirmed that the slope was fierce, but as it was only around one hundred feet to the ledge and the cave, determined men could have manoeuvred the cart up there.

He whispered last instructions to Hearst and Ballard, then headed on a snaking route up the side of the crag.

The dirt was loose and cascaded from under his

feet at every pace, but twenty feet from the top he found a length of deep wheel tracks that Nat and Spenser had failed to mask. He pointed this out to Ballard, who returned a grin then patted Cassidy's back.

In the lead, Cassidy crested the ledge before the cave, although he stayed low. He saw that the ledge was flat and about forty feet wide, the cave nestling under an overhang at the back.

Cassidy ducked below the ledge then directed Hearst and Ballard to hide by a large sentinel rock, the only cover before the cave.

Then he edged down the slope and paced sideways below the cave and out of the view of anyone who was inside, until he was beyond it. Then he climbed the crag, aiming to emerge on the overhang above the cave.

Sure enough, when he crested the top of the crag, he could look down on the flat ledge before the cave and the rock behind which Ballard and Hearst were hiding.

But he could also see the cart, set in a hollow beside the cave.

Cassidy shuffled down the side of the overhang to sit above the mouth of the cave. From this position, he confirmed that the crate wasn't on the back of the cart, but scuffed earth marked its progress into the cave.

Leaning back, so that he kept one hand on the rough rock, Cassidy edged down the side of the overhang. He picked each foothold with care, ensuring that he didn't loosen any stones.

When he'd clambered to twenty feet above the cave entrance, he saw Nat hunkering down behind the cart, looking to the plains.

But Cassidy reckoned that from Nat's low position he couldn't see the place where they had stopped to consider the end of the wheel tracks.

So, there was a good chance he was unaware that they were now closing on him.

Cassidy gestured to the sentinel rock where Hearst and Ballard were hiding, receiving a short wave from Hearst, then edged down the overhang to stand on the edge, directly above the side of the cave entrance and above Nat.

But as he settled down, a dangling foot dislodged a stone.

With slow inevitability, the stone rolled down the last two feet of rock face, then tumbled from the edge, dust and pebbles accompanying it in its short journey to land a yard from Nat's right foot.

Nat flinched, but then looked up, his gaze arcing up the side of the cave towards Cassidy and, in a sudden decision, Cassidy leapt from the overhang. He threw his hands up as he hurtled by the cave entrance, then slammed into Nat's back.

From fifteen feet up, he flattened Nat, the action disorientating himself for a moment. But by the time Nat had regained his senses, Cassidy had shaken his head to clear it and had kicked Nat's gun away.

Cassidy glanced at the cave, confirming that Spenser and Dewey weren't visible, but, as he turned back, Nat swirled round, his fists flailing in a berserk action.

Cassidy took a wild blow to the cheek and another to the chest, but then batted Nat's arms away and grabbed his collar in a firm grip.

Nat struggled, his head lolling and his rolling eyes suggesting he was still unsure as to who had assaulted him, but Cassidy swung him round to face him. He stared deep into his eyes, Nat flinching as his eyes focused, then threw him on his back.

Nat looked up at Cassidy, his eyes wide, but Cassidy paced forward to stand over him. He pulled his gun and aimed it down at his chest.

'Nathaniel,' he muttered, 'you are under arrest.'

Nat raised his hands, then shook his head and when it stopped moving, his eyes were clear. He smiled.

'Howdy, Cassidy,' he said, his voice light and untroubled. 'You took longer than I expected to find me.'

CHAPTER 20

Although Nat remained silent after his initial comment, Cassidy already feared the full story. With a sickness in his guts, he beckoned for Ballard and Hearst to join him.

While he guarded Nat, the two lawmen dashed across the flat area before the cave. Then, on Cassidy's directions, they stalked into the cave, flanking either side.

But within a minute, they'd explored the small recess and they'd confirmed that the crate was in the cave, but it contained only the furs.

The gold shipment had gone, as had Spenser and Dewey.

Cassidy didn't bother questioning Nat as to where they'd gone, refusing to give him the satisfaction.

Instead, he dragged Nat across the front of the cave and pushed him towards Ballard, who *did* question Nat. But Nat refused to talk other than to state repeatedly that when he'd given his word, he never broke it.

But Hearst found Nat's horse, then found tracks for a second cart, which had been in the cave. The tracks led south.

So, Ballard relented from his interrogation and bound Nat. Then, with Ballard holding him in a firm grip, they headed down the side of the crag to their horses.

Ballard moved to place Nat on the back of his horse, but he stopped and dragged him back to Cassidy then pushed him forward a pace.

'This one is yours,' he said, his former arrogance gone from his tone as he met Cassidy's gaze.

'This is your territory,' Cassidy said, 'and your prisoner.'

'Yeah, but after all your trouble, I reckon you can deal with him yourself back in Morb . . . back in Monotony.'

Cassidy nodded and took Nat's rope from Ballard.

'And I reckon Spenser and Dewey won't get far. Not with an idiot like Dewey at the reins and a lawman like you after them.'

Ballard slapped his thigh, a huge smile emerging.

'You're right. I'll track them down before they leave my county – just like any outlaw that does wrong on my patch.'

'I don't doubt it,' Cassidy smiled as Ballard headed for his horse. 'But you'd better catch them soon.'

'Why?'

'If you don't, you might stray into another lawman's territory.'

Ballard swung on to his horse. 'That's never worried me before.' He winked and turned his horse to head south.

Cassidy handed the rope to Hearst then considered Nat as his deputy led his new prisoner to his horse. But Nat didn't return his gaze. Cassidy nodded to himself then hailed Ballard.

Ballard padded his horse back to stand over Cassidy.

'I know where the gold is,' Cassidy said.

Ballard glanced over Cassidy's shoulder at Nat.

'Because you understand the way that outlaw's mind works?'

Cassidy sighed. 'Nope. I now have to admit that I don't understand him. I understand the likes of Spenser and Dewey more.'

Ballard nodded. 'What's your hunch?'

'They use misdirection.'

'You saying that the tracks from the second cart led south, so that means they went somewhere else?'

'Yeah. You could chase phantom tracks for weeks and not find them because Spenser and Dewey will go to the last place you'd expect them to go.'

'Like the place they've been camping for the last week?'

'That's the idea. But there's somewhere even more unlikely for them to go: Deadman's Gulch where your deputies arrested Rodrigo Fernandez.'

'Because that's the last place anybody would hide out,' Ballard mused.

Ballard and Cassidy exchanged a nod and a grin. Then Ballard headed back to Deadman's Gulch, leaving Cassidy and Hearst alone with Nat.

'Come on, Hearst,' Cassidy said, turning to his horse. 'We got an outlaw to take in.'

Hearst nodded and bundled Nat on to his horse, then mounted his own steed and secured the rope.

'You got anything to say about that?' Hearst said, tugging Nat's rope.

Nat glanced at Hearst, nothing in his firm gaze suggesting to Cassidy that his hunch was correct. But as Cassidy no longer understood Nat's attitude, that meant nothing.

Nat turned in the saddle to face Cassidy, then smiled.

'Don't blame me, Cassidy,' he said.

'And keep a tight hold of that rope, Hearst,' Cassidy said as he reached his horse. 'I don't want no trouble from our prisoner.'

'Cassidy,' Nat said, 'you can't ignore me for ever.'

'And make sure our prisoner doesn't waste his breath talking.'

'You heard him,' Hearst said, pulling the rope binding him to Nat taut and dragging Nat back in the saddle.

'Cassidy,' Nat said, righting himself, 'I kept my promises to you.'

Cassidy mounted his horse and lifted the reins, but then lowered them and glared at Nat.

'You did nothing,' he muttered.

'Rodrigo Fernandez is dead. I've handed myself in. And Spenser has the gold shipment.'

Cassidy looked over his shoulder to see Ballard disappear over the ridge and into Deadman's Gulch.

'Whether my hunch about your plans was right or wrong, with that lawman on his trail, Spenser won't enjoy his gold for long.'

'Either way, I still kept my promises.'

'You're forgotten so much of what I taught you that

you don't know what promises mean no more,' Cassidy snapped, then shook the reins, moving his horse on.

Cassidy rode from the crag, Hearst and the trailing Nat ahead of him, but as they passed the end of the cart tracks, he pulled back on the reins. Leaning from the saddle, he stared at the tracks then closed his eyes, envisaging the other tracks that Hearst had found on the ledge.

'Misdirection,' he whispered to himself. 'The tracks from the second cart weren't there to confuse us as to the direction they took. They were there to make us believe there *was* a second cart.'

Cassidy snorted, swung his horse round, and hurtled towards the crag.

'Where you going?' Hearst shouted, swirling round in the saddle.

'Just guard our prisoner,' Cassidy shouted over his shoulder.

At a gallop, he reached the crag. His horse balked at the incline, but Cassidy jumped down and scurried, on hands and feet, up the slope to reach the flat ledge before the cave.

He stood and stalked towards the cave, his gun drawn. With his gaze darting about the crag, he wandered round the cart to consider the tracks that the second cart had made. They were identical to the other cart tracks.

With his gun held low, he entered the cave, then ripped the lid from the crate and dragged the furs from within, hurling them to the ground as he confirmed nobody was hiding inside.

In the cave entrance, he ran his gaze over the

ledge. The ground was rocky, but in a hollow before the cave, sand had collected. And ten feet before the cave, an animal bone, possibly hollow, protruded from the ground.

Cassidy smiled, then paced on to the sand.

Something snagged his leg and pulled him to his knees. He swirled round to see that a hand had emerged from the sand and grabbed his ankle.

Then Spenser rose from the ground, sand cascading from his form. But Spenser was slow in dragging himself free, giving Cassidy enough time to rip his leg away and clip Spenser's jaw.

Spenser shrugged off the blow. On his back, he grabbed Cassidy's collar and kicked up to wheel Cassidy over his head.

Cassidy landed on his back and lay stunned, enabling Spenser to stand then dive at him. But Cassidy rolled to the side, Spenser's dive landing him on his belly and, as Spenser floundered, Cassidy jumped to his feet. He ripped back his foot and kicked out, the blow crunching into the point of Spenser's chin and cracking his head back.

As Spenser slumped, unconscious, footfalls pounded behind him.

Cassidy half-swirled round, but the sand-coated Dewey hurtled into his side and flattened him. On the ground, Cassidy squirmed, attempting to extricate himself, but Dewey drew his gun and aimed it at Cassidy's head.

'Don't,' Cassidy grunted.

'And don't push me,' Dewey muttered, as he stood and loomed over Cassidy. 'I just want to better myself. And the gold will do that.'

'After the life you've led, even jail will better your life. But shooting me will just end it.'

With the back of his left hand, Dewey wiped his mouth, his gaze flickering between the sprawled Spenser and a spot near the cave, leading Cassidy to assume that that was where they'd hidden the gold.

'I'll take my chances.'

'You won't,' Hearst shouted from the end of the ledge. 'You are under arrest, Dewey.'

Dewey flinched, but then backed two paces with his gun still aimed down at Cassidy.

Cassidy shuffled to a sitting position and glanced over his shoulder. Hearst had Nat's rope slung over his shoulder, dragging Nat along, five paces back.

Dewey rolled his shoulders, then firmed his gun hand.

'I'm takin' the gold or dyin',' he roared.

Two gunshots blasted.

A slug whistled by Cassidy's head and gouged into the dirt beside his right ear as Dewey wheeled to the ground, clutching his shoulder. Cassidy rolled to his feet and pounded three long paces to kick Dewey's gun away, then turned, but it was to see Hearst lying flat on his belly and Nat dashing over the end of the ledge.

Hearst stumbled to his feet, rubbing the back of his head, and moved to follow Nat, but Cassidy ordered him to guard the wounded Dewey and the unconscious Spenser instead, and dashed past him.

When he reached the end of the ledge, Nat was already halfway down the slope, his rope trailing behind him. As Cassidy's horse was now mooching twenty yards from the crag bottom, Cassidy hurtled headlong down the slope after him, but even though the rope binding Nat's wrists impeded his running, Nat was still a full thirty feet ahead.

Cassidy bounded down the slope, his feet slipping on the loose stones, but Nat slipped, too, and, with his bound hands not letting him stop himself from falling, he tumbled down to the flat earth.

Nat lay a moment, shook his head, then staggered to his feet but, as he set off, Cassidy dived the last ten feet and thudded into Nat's shoulders, his momentum dragging Nat to the ground.

Cassidy and Nat tumbled for five feet, then slammed to a halt. But Cassidy rolled to his knees first and pole-axed Nat with a clip to the jaw then dragged Nat to his feet. With anger ripping through his guts, he stood Nat straight and pummelled his cheek with a left hook that knocked him one way then with a round-armed slug that knocked him the other way.

Nat crashed to the ground, ploughing through the dirt before he halted, but Cassidy was on him in a moment and ripping back his fist ready to pummel him again.

Nat peered up at Cassidy, dirt and blood streaking his face.

'Cassidy, stop!' he shouted. 'It's me, Nat.'

'Yeah, you are Nat,' Cassidy grunted. He slugged Nat's jaw, then grabbed the trailing rope and dragged him to his feet. 'But whoever you answer to, you're heading to the same place.'